THE
GIFTS OF KALI

Also by Lou Paduano

The Greystone Saga

Signs of Portents
Tales from Portents
The Medusa Coin
Pathways in the Dark
A Circle of Shadows

Greystone-in-Training

Hammer and Anvil

The DSA

Season One
The Clearing
Promethean
The Bridge
Spectral Advocate
Dark Impulses
Broken Loyalties

THE
GIFTS OF KALI

Greystone-in-Training Book Two

Lou Paduano

Eleven Ten Publishing LLC

GRAND ISLAND, NEW YORK

Eleven Ten Publishing LLC
282 Fareway Lane
Grand Island, NY 14072

Publisher's note: This is a work of fiction. Names, characters, places, and incidents either are the product of the author's imagination or are used fictitiously. Any resemblance to actual events, locales, or persons, living or dead, is entirely coincidental.

Printed in the United States of America
Edited by JD Book Services
Cover art design by MiblArt

First edition published 2020

Library of Congress Cataloguing in Publication Data
Paduano, Lou
The Gifts of Kali / Lou Paduano

LCCN: 2020909684
ISBN-13: 978-1-944965-66-2 (hardcover)
ISBN-13: 978-1-944965-30-3 (paperback)
ISBN-13: 978-1-944965-29-7 (eBook)

To Bob and Louise,
for the very special gift they gave me.

CHAPTER ONE

The operation went like clockwork. The shipment had been lost in the midst of a small, violent outbreak along the borders of no less than four third-world countries. An enterprising soul found the missing cargo crates filled with weapons in the ruins of a firefight and contacted some friends across the Atlantic. He managed to have the shipment smuggled on a small freighter that took them down the Mediterranean and into open waters.

They were free and clear before a shred of paperwork had been written over the incident. To the military, the supplies had been destroyed in the conflict—possibly even due to their own bombing of the area. It was a fact no one wanted in the media, so it was suppressed and forgotten.

The right payoffs had made their way into the hands of customs officials at the port on the east side of Portents. A covered maintenance slip had been reserved for the delivery, and the ship had come in under the cover of night into the waiting hands of the crew ready for their payday.

Devon Little had been waiting for his for over two decades. He carried a job as an administrator for a local bank—he made peanuts but kept his head down and was therefore viewed as valuable to the company. He had even been promoted for his minimal efforts. It kept him occupied when his *real* work ran dry.

Petty theft. Gun running. Protection schemes. He and his crew were versatile in their work. They rarely let an opportunity pass by, so when a colleague in the Army reached out, he was ready, willing, and able to see the deal through to the end.

It was the one—the final score to set him up for life. It would give his children and their children the best of everything. Cost would no longer be an issue. There would be no more small-time jobs, no more slaving away for his 401k.

Devon would finally have it all.

The shipment arrived unmolested by any officials and his crew was there for the delivery. Geoff and Dougie took the lead. They removed the arms from the hidden compartment below deck. Placing each item in crates, the crew catalogued everything for the buyer Devon had lined up weeks earlier.

Automatic weapons, sniper rifles, grenades, even landmines were part of the deal. Each crate contained enough product to go for seven figures. There were twelve crates and six men on the team—a nice, easy split of over two million dollars each once the job was completed.

Devon acted as a lookout. There was always the chance of outside interference. A payoff might have been seen as too little, or a better deal might have sprung up by a third-party source. Hell, there was even the chance the cops might have caught wind of their smuggling, but with each passing minute that seemed less and less likely.

"Hey," he called to Geoff, who was overseeing the packaging. "Make sure they're careful with that crate."

Geoff grinned, then approached. A cigarette sat on his lips, and he puffed it casually. "Relax, Dev. We're all here for the same thing."

"I know," Devon said. He shook off the stress of it, pushed aside the tension that came in tandem with his excitement. It was almost too good to be true. "This is it, man. This is the big one for us."

"Thank Christ the Domingos ain't around no more, eh?"

Frank Domingo had once been the man who ruled the street gangs in Portents. Nothing was done without his approval. Devon and his friends had found themselves under Frank's heel more often than not, working for a pittance while the Italian-loafer-wearing goomba cleaned up from their hard labor. When the indictments came down ending Frank's reign, Devon had hosted a party at his place.

Dougie stopped near the door. He carried a pair of Colt M16A2 rifles. "They were nothing but greedy bloodsuckers. To hell with all of 'em."

"This one is ours," Devon said with a smile. It caused the scar on his chin to stretch across his cheek. Dougie handed him one of the rifles. They were military grade, all right, but the serial numbers had been defaced. They were untraceable.

"The buyer?" Geoff asked.

"He's flying in tomorrow morning," Devon replied. "We make the deal here at midnight."

Geoff took the automatic weapon in hand and raised it over his head. "And buy our first beachfront property the next day."

Devon laughed. "Something like that."

Dougie took the gun back, then passed the pair off to the others, who continued to pack the crates. He held out a hand to Geoff. A roll of the eyes was Geoff's standard answer to the gesture, but he relented and passed along a cigarette to the waiting man. Dougie pulled out his lighter and settled along the frame next to Devon.

"You still worried, Dev?"

"Trying not to be."

"Good," Dougie said. He patted the man's shoulder. "Gotta put those kids through college, right?"

Devon had four of the ankle-biters at home. His wife couldn't get enough of them. He had never had the family-man gene in him before he met her. Over time, though, he had grown to appreciate the joy children brought to his home. They were all he thought of now.

"Exactly," Devon said. He stared out into the quiet of the docks. The port stretched up the coast, which was mostly emptied due to the late-winter weather. The ice had broken weeks earlier and slowly drifted out of the harbor to allow their transport to arrive unhindered. To Devon, the solitude of the dock was peaceful—almost serene.

Suddenly, a sharp streak of green light soared across the sky. It started at the middle of the port and sailed overhead for miles to the north. Everyone at the slip stopped what they were doing. Six men crowded around the door for a better look.

Geoff pushed ahead. His cigarette fell to the ground and he stamped it out. "What the hell was that?"

Devon held him back and pointed to the gear scattered across the deck. "You guys finish unloading. We need to make sure everything is ready for tomorrow night."

Geoff's brow furrowed. "You sure you don't want me to come with you?"

"It's probably nothing," Devon answered with the shake of his head. "I'll be right back."

Protests rose from Dougie and Geoff, but Devon refused to listen. He started out of the covered dock to check out the streak that had faded as quickly as it had arrived.

The waterfront was quiet and a fog settled in with the late hour. It covered his movements. It also obscured the path ahead.

From between two storage units, which were used for cleaning equipment and long-term parking for some of the high-end clientele who frequented the port, came a figure rushing into the night. Devon could tell it was a woman from her slight figure. She wore a green cloak. The hood did its best to cover her scarlet locks.

"Not again," he heard her say as she fled from the area.

"Hello?" Devon called out.

"It isn't right," she cried. Her words faded just like her presence. "I failed. Again."

He tried to catch her, but she broke into a run. "What are you—?"

Devon stopped between the buildings where the woman had been. He meant to keep going, to find out if she was in the area because of their operation. He had to know if they were at risk. But at that moment, a light cut through the fog from deep between the storage units.

"What the hell?"

Devon stepped deeper, winding his way through a series of crates, until the light took shape. It was a door—free-standing away from any structure. The light grew from its center. Devon approached cautiously. His hand ran along his back to where his pistol was secured. He suddenly wished the others *had* come along.

A figure stepped out of the light emanating from the door. He stood tall and proud, his torso was completely naked, and his legs were covered by a pair of white pants. His skin beamed in a pale bluish hue. He stopped once free from the door and stared through the light to where he had come from.

"Hey, pal," Devon said. "You can't be here."

"I can't? Yet here I am," he said, his voice confident. He continued to stare into the piercing light. Devon couldn't make out any details within the strange portal. "This is the world, isn't it? The physical world? I'm here after so long."

"What... who are you?" Devon asked. He stumbled forward, curiosity overtaking common sense. He snapped back when he heard the approach of steps behind him.

"Dev, is everything all right?"

The rest of the crew had joined him. Dougie and Geoff held tight to the military-grade arms they sought to sell. The others stayed back, however, more terrified than curious.

"Who the heck is this guy?" Geoff asked. He huffed and approached the man, who still focused more on where he had been than the threat at his back.

"Geoff," Devon said. "I wouldn't—"

Geoff shook his head and primed his sidearm. "I can handle this refugee from a horror flick. Now beat it, buddy, before I—"

No one noticed the sword against the man's back. They never saw the stranger pull it free from its sheath or slice the air where Geoff stood. They only saw their friend fall with a deep cut across his chest.

"GEOFF!" Devon yelled.

The man held the blade up. The steel darkened to black, and the stranger ran his finger over the obsidian.

"Ah, the fresh taint of sin," he said. His eyes were all white and they seemed to glow in the shadows of the dock. "Exactly what I was looking for."

"Dear God," Devon whispered.

The man approached, the sword at his side. "Close enough."

Devon failed to move. He heard the cries of the others, especially the rage from Dougie over the death of their friend, but he couldn't follow his crew as they raced toward the stranger. He could only watch as they were slaughtered, each in turn, by the man's sword. Devon was unable to move, unable to believe his final score had slipped through his fingers just as quickly as his life was taken from him.

CHAPTER TWO

The music boomed throughout the bar. The jukebox—on its last legs—was scratchy with its rendition of a pop song long forgotten by most of the crowd. The woman dancing between three young men in the middle of the open floor knew every word. She screamed them with a smile on her face and a beer in her hand. With each repetition of the chorus she lifted her glass to the air and joined the others in a drink.

The Town Hall Pub was not known for its revelry. Most of the patrons were aged men who wanted nothing more than somber silence in which to drown their memories away for the night. Once a week that changed for the establishment. Once a week, the woman named Callie stopped in for a visit.

She changed the entire dynamic of the bar. Young men started to frequent the place. They hung around the electronic dart boards that rarely worked and the one pool table with a thick scratch that tended to block the corner pocket along the green felt surface. They came in the hopes of seeing Callie, of being next to her through her renditions of songs few knew, or hearing her laughter when offered free drinks and more.

Callie rubbed against the man to her left, who seemed to be the leader of the pack. The song reached a crescendo, sending them all into a frenzy. They hopped like mad on the makeshift dance floor and sang at the tops of their lungs. The world around them was nothing more than a blur. Everyone stared at Callie. She was the center of their universe whenever she was in the room.

When the song ended cries erupted for more. The men

wanted her close. They wanted to feel the life that seemed to beam from her surface. But in the silent aftermath of the dance, Callie pulled away. Hands grabbed for her and gifts were offered for another second of her company.

"Soon, boys," she cooed. Her wide eyes washed over them all, always careful not to focus too long on an individual. They might have known her name, but she couldn't tell them apart. They were merely there for her in whatever capacity she demanded for the night. "I'll be back soon."

An argument wasn't necessary and none took root. The group of enthusiastic man candy returned to the dart boards and their waiting pitchers of beer. Callie headed for the bar. Her hand grazed the shoulders of the older gents slumped in their seats. Each touch brought a smile to their lips. She continued to the far side, under the dim lights, and sat.

The bartender was in front of her before she could even ask. She might not have known the names of her dancing companions, but she would have been remiss to ignore the man with the keys to the liquor. George had been the only bartender she'd ever seen at the Town Hall Pub.

He grabbed the bottle of tequila and filled a glass. "Callie."

The name widened her grin. She didn't know why it mattered to her, but when she heard it from those around her, it brought her a sick sense of joy. She took the shot and swallowed it down. The glass settled on the bar before her, her nail tapping lightly along the lip.

"Another one, Georgie."

"I don't think that's what you want," he said.

She raised an eyebrow at him and waited. "Come on, George. I can take it."

"I know you can, girl," George replied. He shook the bottle of booze before her. It was almost drained. "It's my tequila that has trouble keeping up."

He lowered the bottle on the bar and she snatched it. Callie poured a shot, then downed the searing liquid with a gulp. She set the glass before him. George grumbled and reached for the booze. Callie put another twenty on the bar next to the glass. With a sigh, he pocketed the cash and left the bottle in front of her.

She poured the next round and held it in front of the face in the mirror at the back of the bar. The glass obscured her image, splitting it as she squinted through the liquor.

George swiped at the bar with a stained rag and watched as she finished another shot. "You come in here once a week. Always solo. You make a big splash, stir up all kinds of trouble from the boys even though you have zero interest in any of them. You don't really talk to anyone except me, and that's only to get your fill of my liquor. You're young, beautiful, could have your run of the place with anyone or anything you want. So what's your story, Callie?"

"No story to tell," she said. She had never answered that question, not in all the years it'd been asked. Stories came with endings. She preferred to just keep living. "I hate to get bogged down in the details—"

"—so why bother to offer any." George said, finishing her thought.

"More fun that way," Callie admitted. She played with the ribbon at her wrist. It was pink and snaked up her left arm to her elbow. She picked at the tightly tied knot, feeling the warmth of the fabric against the cold of the night. "The living's all that matters."

George nodded. He filled his own glass and joined her for another round. A question settled on his lips. His curiosity was bordering on pestering. Before he had the chance a bright light filled the room.

"What the hell?" George asked. He hobbled to the end of the bar. Patrons rushed for the windows lining the front of the establishment. The streak of light shot across the way before disappearing from view, and then the calm returned to the night.

"You see that?" one of the patrons asked.

"Strangest damn thing," another commented.

The first man shook his head. "Whole city is getting strange, you ask me."

George turned back to Callie, who stood from her stool. Her eyes locked on the window and the quiet of the docks outside. The green hue of the light brought back a distant memory.

"What is it, kiddo?" George asked, clearly able to see the concern on her face. "You seen something like that before?"

She poured a final shot. "Not in a long time."

Callie downed the drink and placed the glass on the bar before George.

"Callie…"

"Thanks for the drink, George," she said without looking at him.

"Everything all right, kid?" he called after her.

"Always," Callie said with a smile and a wave. "I'll see you soon."

The light was still caught in her eyes. It blinded her thoughts and caused her to collide with one of her former dancing partners from earlier in the evening.

"Whoa there, beautiful," he said, blocking the front door. He caught her wrist, and his gaze washed over her entire body in an instant. "Where you headed in such a hurry?"

"Out," she said. She pulled away from him, but he stuck close. Her answer had done nothing to satisfy his appetite.

"Want some company?"

"Not at all."

He continued to block the door when she tried to push through. His hand settled on her arm this time, tighter than before. "Come on, you don't mean that. Not after all the fun we've had already."

One of the man's friends at a nearby table shuffled over. He held out a set of darts for the game that had been interrupted by the strange light. "Ed, come on. I wouldn't—"

Callie grinned and leaned close. "Yeah, Ed. I wouldn't—" Her fingers danced up his arm and his grip slackened.

"Now, that's what I—"

Her hand stopped at the back of his head, and then she slammed it down with all her force. Ed's face collided against the tabletop next to them. Blood smeared the solid oak from the impact. Callie let Ed go and backed away for the door. His friend rushed to his side, while Ed covered up his nose which freely poured blood down his face.

"My nose!" he cried. "She broke my—"

Her laughter carried her from the bar. She didn't have to hear another word. Joy followed her steps down the pier and her concern faded away. Life mattered, free and unencumbered. Fun was what it all boiled down to when it came to living.

The Town Hall Pub sat in a derelict corner of the harbor. It was forgotten, like many of the early days of Portents. Few traveled in that direction, not with the red-light districts of downtown or the more sophisticated—and safer—aspects of the coves. Callie roamed the docks alone. She was free in Portents, content to go wherever the wind took her. She regretted the wind's choice of destinations that night.

Bodies lay on the ground. Guns rested in their grip or at their side. Bullet holes dotted the buildings and cargo containers around them. There had been a fight, but the weapons had obviously done little to save the poor fools before her.

"Great," Callie muttered as she crept closer to the gap between buildings. "A perfectly good buzz ruined by my own curiosity."

She stopped at the edge of the first building. It was a storage warehouse for the docks. There were a dozen of the same type staggered up and down the entire port. A dim light glowed between the two closest to her position. She crept around the corner and through a series of crates for a better look.

The light shone in the shape of a door. A green hue emanated from the surface. "That light," Callie said. "I've seen that light before. But where—?"

A shadow fell over the door and a figure stepped into view. He carried another body with one hand. He emptied the dead man's pockets. There was a curious look on his face as he took the victim's cash. He tucked the bills away, then dropped his victim at his feet. He surveyed the death around him.

"Oh, no," Callie whispered.

She covered her mouth, cursing her loose lips. When the figure's white eyes started to turn in her direction, she ran. She reached the far side of the building, and ducked for cover behind another row of crates. Her body trembled with fear and she shut her eyes tight.

Wood creaked on the other side of her shelter. The sound of

scraping metal ran along the wooden lids above her. Then the sound faded, and the steps along with it.

When she shifted from her cover, the figure was gone. Callie slid down the side of the closest crate, and tucked her knees in close. She was terrified at what the man's arrival meant for her and for the future she had dared to ignore for so long.

"No," she whispered in the cold of the night. "Not him. Not now."

But it was him. There was no denying it.

Shiva had come to Portents.

CHAPTER THREE

He hadn't meant to ask the question. For hours, Mentor had sat in meditation before the glowing green light of the Bypass. His work had always demanded clarity of thought, a pure will to seek answers from the infinite crossroad that stretched beyond the veil of the floating globe.

It hovered in the center of four marble pillars. Each was etched with glyphs, letters, and runes from languages long since lost to the world. They locked the Bypass in place and protected it from outside influence. They also served to protect Mentor, to warn him of the possible dangers within the mysterious artifact.

He had been more tired than usual. Ever since his run-in with the Minotaur, his body had ached for more sleep than usual. His right knee continued to bother him, and he had taken to resting in the afternoon where once he could go days without proper sleep. The work had caught up with him, but he soldiered on.

When Soriya had asked him for assistance in looking into a case, he had agreed. More and more often, her training took place outside the chamber walls. She was more the Greystone these days than him, working tirelessly to take down the constant wave of threats that hid within Portents.

He worried about her still. He always would, but he had reconciled that concern. She was needed, and he would be there to support her. Be it at her side or at their home, gazing into the void of time and space for answers, he did what he could to assist her.

Unfortunately, the worry—combined with his exhaustion—

led him astray. His knee had locked up from the hours of sitting so still. Pain shot up his leg and he instinctively reached for the stone. The Greystone cooled him and soothed his wound. It had been with him for so long while keeping him safe from the world, he feared the day it would leave him completely.

That was when he saw the end. That was when the Bypass had taken his worry, his concern for the future, and showed it to him. Mentor witnessed the future right before his eyes.

He saw his death.

He hadn't meant to ask, never meant to know, but the vision had come through the Bypass. It offered no definitive date, no clear name to the threat that broke his body and tossed him aside as if he were nothing. All the Bypass could do was show him the mismatched eyes of his killer—one a cold blue and the other blood red.

Mentor turned away from the Bypass after that. He dropped the stone to his side and fought to stand. He had never considered the brutality of his end. For years, he had stood against the threats in Portents. He had trained Soriya to take over for him, but not until she was better prepared. She was too young to be burdened by the task ahead. He was meant to be there for her throughout—the way he had been taught so many years ago.

Thoughts of Soriya spurred him back to the small domicile tucked in the corner of the expansive chamber. There were four rooms built out of the wall. Two bedrooms, a living area with a fireplace, and a bathroom. He stopped in front of his student's room. Her bed was a mess with clothes scattered across the floor. She came home to sleep and eat mostly. There had been little in the way of downtime for them of late.

Mentor continued to his room and reached beneath the pillow on his bed. He pulled out a small box hidden there and held it close. Opening the lid, Mentor removed the gold locket inside.

He had kept it safe for over a decade. The locket had been passed to him with the hope it would make its way to its true owner at some point. He had never found a good time; the right moment had never presented itself for him to explain the truth to Soriya. He should have shared everything with her long ago. There were answers he should have passed along right from the start.

Carefully, Mentor slipped the locket back into the box. He closed the lid and carried the gift to the mantel. There, he placed the locket into another box and tied a ribbon around it. A red bow sat on top.

Tomorrow he would tell her the truth—from the locket to the vision he had witnessed in the Bypass. Both truths frightened him, but she had to know. Soriya was the heir to the Greystone mantle. She would have to be. All choice had been taken out of the equation thanks to the question he never meant to ask. *None* of them had any choice left in the matter.

Fate had taken over.

CHAPTER FOUR

The neon lights of the Petrov Animal Shelter flickered and buzzed with dimming intensity. The shop was closed, and the sign had all but fallen from the sticky tab on the glass of the front door.

Soriya Greystone reached for the handle and pulled. The door was locked. She glanced at her companion, who huffed under his breath. His hand replaced hers. The lock snapped under his grasp and the door slid from the frame with ease.

"I could have done that," Soriya commented.

Urg's nostrils flared with contempt as he continued into the shop. Soriya smirked at his discomfort. He didn't want to be here. As a seven-foot-tall orc with light green skin, he didn't like to go out of his way to cause trouble.

Yet that was exactly why Soriya had asked him to come along this evening. They ducked down and shuffled across the shelter. A rectangular window ran the length of the back wall of the lobby, and it offered a view of the kennels and pens for the animals kept for their protection or to find a new home. The pair stayed low and hugged close to the wall.

Urg groaned when he looked to his watch. "I'm going to be late for work."

"What?" she asked as she swiped the hair from her face.

Urg lifted the cuff of his tailored suit jacket and held up his watch. "I have to work tonight."

"You didn't have to come, Urg," she said, though she knew the second she'd mentioned her visit to the shop he would accompany her. He had been protective of her ever since they'd met on the street when she was seven. At the time, she only knew him as the 'green monster.' She had gone out of her way to visit when she had been allowed to leave the sanctuary of the Bypass with Mentor. Urg always claimed to dislike the name, though she would sometimes catch his smile when she said it.

Urg played with his collar, which caused the spikes in his neck to poke out from beneath his pressed shirt. His yellow eyes bored through her. "And leave you to handle this on your own? What kind of orc would I be to let that happen?"

"I don't even know how to answer that question," she said. A confused look passed from him. "You're my one and only orc, Urg."

He grinned. "Well, I'd like to think my brethren would do the same, but alas, they'd probably feast on your flesh. Possibly even cook you alive. A nice stew, perhaps."

"A nice stew, huh?" she asked. "That sounds kinda good right now."

"You say that, until you find yourself boiled alive with nothing but regrets."

Soriya chuckled under her breath. "Well, then, I am glad that *you're* here instead."

Urg had always known how to make her smile. It was part of his charm, and it was why when she was forced to stay in the Courtyard for weeks on end as a child she'd always sought him out. She looked to him as a friend, a confidant to talk to about the world they lived in. He was one of the specials that had come to Portents looking to start a life—to be part of the world instead of separate from it. Urg was also one of the few to make a real go of it, with a job as a bouncer at a local club. He put in the effort and was rewarded for it. Few did when it came to the myths and legends that seemed to crop up in the city constantly.

The beast in the back room of the shelter was the perfect example. Soriya peeked through the glass, careful to stay out of sight. Amid the domestic pets waiting for new owners stood a Tengu. The creature appeared to be male, with the body of a human. The head, however, was that of a giant predatory bird with stark black eyes and a long beak. The Tengu snapped open a cage, pulled the resident—a cute hamster—out, and dangled it over his maw.

Soriya inched up, ready to start the fight. The beast caught sight of movement in the corner of its eye and spun in her direction. She dropped back down to the ground and held her breath. The creature's shadow loomed over them and its nails tapped along the window. Soriya put a finger to her lips while she pressed even tighter to the wall. Urg tried to do the same, his bulk not quite made for skulking. When they heard the Tengu munching on his appetizer, they figured it was safe once again.

Soriya had been hunting the creature for the better part of a week. There had been a rash of break-ins at shelters across Portents. All had reported the same: no robbery, only the slaughter of a few small animals. They had been fed on. Police chalked it up to a lunatic, but Soriya read the signs better. She knew what had somehow made its way into her city—and she knew how to deal with it.

It was Urg, though, that had informed her about Petrov Animal Shelter as a possible target. So when she had decided to head over, she'd felt she owed the big lug a chance to tackle the problem with her.

Soriya patted his shoulder and tilted her head to the back room door. "Ready?"

He stood up next to the window and she followed suit. The hamster was gone. Stray tufts of fur floated in the air. The animals screeched and wailed for assistance as the Tengu circled the cages, looking for the next course of his meal. Urg ran his hands over his pristine suit.

"I didn't bring a change of clothes."

"So?"

"So, I have work," Urg said.

Soriya smirked. "You'll be fine. Trust me."

"It worries me when you say that."

"You've got this," she said. "Come on."

When they reached the door, she stopped. He took the handle and nodded to her. She counted to three, then bolted back to the front of the shop.

They came in with a plan of attack. Urg's job was to frighten the Tengu, an easy enough task for the towering orc. Once threatened, the beast would only have one exit: the back of the shop and then the alley connecting it to the street. Soriya rounded the building and took up position at the mouth of the shallow alley.

She didn't have to wait for long. The door smashed outward and slammed against the brick edifice. The Tengu screeched, animals yowling in the background. Soriya stood her ground with a smirk on her lips.

"And that's how a plan comes together."

Soriya leapt at the beast. Her fist connected with its beak and the monster reeled away at the last second to roll with the blow. She followed it up with a roundhouse kick, which drove the Tengu back.

"The buffet is closed for you, birdie."

The Tengu squawked a loud and inhuman sound. The creature's arms spread wide. Its skin split, as if sliced open by a large knife. Feathers grew into wings thick and dark.

"Oh, that is just gross." Soriya jumped at the beast, who reacted instinctively. All force went to its wings. It flapped them with a frenzied fury, kicking up a gale-force wind. Soriya lost all momentum and was blown back from the intensity of the gust. She crashed against the brick, and her shoulder hit hard when she fell to the concrete.

She tried to pick herself back up, fighting to focus as the wind pummeled her. She blinked rapidly to shake off the shock of the blow.

The Tengu loomed overhead. A victory screech arose, as did its fists.

Then the sound cut out. The screeching halted and the beast's arms fell limp at its side. The head of the Tengu slumped to the side then fell to the ground, right before its entire body collapsed.

"What the hell?"

Behind the crumpled corpse of the Tengu stood a woman with wild, black hair and wide purple eyes. She carried no blade, which shocked Soriya even more than her presence. Instead, she held a ribbon which was wrapped tight at one end to her left wrist.

"How did you—?"

"Relax," the woman said with a smug grin. "I've got this one."

CHAPTER FIVE

Soriya took the woman's extended hand and found her way to her feet. She couldn't stop staring. The woman looked to be no older than her mid-twenties. Tattoos marked her right arm. Her left was bare except for the ribbon tied to her wrist, which snaked along her forearm. Her smile gave her a hint of danger and intrigue that Soriya found fascinating.

"You okay?" the woman asked. She cocked an eyebrow, clearly uncomfortable with Soriya's gawking.

Soriya shook her head then backed away slightly. "Who are you? How did you—?"

The ribbon wriggled along the woman's wrist. She tucked her arm behind her back and out of view. "I was in the area and saw the fracas. Thought maybe I could help." Soriya continued to wait for more. "Callie. That's my name, since you asked. And you are?"

"Soriya."

Callie grinned. "I like it. And your moves. Do this often?"

She stepped around the decapitated corpse of the Tengu. "More than you'd think." She rubbed her shoulder. "Usually with better results."

"Soriya!" The scream carried through the alley and drew them to the doorway. Three yipping puppies raced by them, and a handful of birds soared into the night sky. Behind the escaping animals stood Urg.

"It's all good, Urg. It's done." Soriya said.

His suit jacket was torn in thick strips and there was excrement along his shoulders, down his right pant leg, and on his shoes. He nearly stumbled through the doorway, but held to the frame for support as another dog slipped past him.

Soriya struggled to suppress a laugh. "What happened to *you?*"

"Nothing." Urg cleared his throat as he looked around and straightened his jacket. "I don't want to talk about it."

A curious look escaped Callie, who sauntered over to the disheveled figure. She ran a hand over her chin. "An orc? Interesting."

He huffed at her examination.

Soriya's arms crossed her chest. "His name is Urg. An old friend."

"And you are?" Urg said in a deep voice. Typically, an orc brought a certain level of intimidation to anyone in their vicinity. Callie didn't appear fazed in the least. She didn't flinch at the sound of his voice or the imposing nature of his bulky frame.

"Callie," she answered. "A new friend."

Urg moved for the dead beast in the alley. "Soriya, how did you—?"

"Wasn't me this time," Soriya replied. She had come to the shelter prepared to take care of the menace. Instead, she'd found herself in danger. Callie had saved her. The woman knew the truth about the city and had the skills to handle the threats unleashed.

Callie hopped atop the closed dumpster in the back of the alley. "We should celebrate!"

Soriya retrieved the head of the Tengu and held it before her. Beady eyes stared back, almost as if it had yet to become aware of its own demise. She moved for the dumpster, and Callie shifted to one side to allow her to lift the lid. The head fell in with a crash. Callie held the lid open as Urg tossed the corpse of the monster inside. He shuffled some bags of trash atop the body to hide it from sight.

No one needed to see what had happened. Few wanted to know about the true city, about what occurred when the sun went down. Most nights were calm and quiet. However, when something arrived from outside the norm, when the myths and legends of old managed to escape into the present, it was safer for the people of Portents to hide indoors.

"What do you think?" Callie asked. She waited for a reply to her tempting invitation.

Soriya, however, knew she was expected back at home. Mentor would be waiting for an update, to learn about the Tengu and see if the situation had truly been handled. Any outside communication was frowned upon, though he had grown to accept Urg's presence when it came to the work—mostly to avoid a fight with Soriya. She took what she could from the stubborn old teacher. Mentor had been through a lot in recent months. His leg was still recovering from the Minotaur's assault, and his time as the Greystone was slowly coming to an end. It had become her job more and more, though the title remained his for as long as he wished.

He needed her more now, though. His reliance was difficult for him to accept, but she shouldered the responsibility. There had been little room for celebrating over the last few months.

"I can't. I have to—"

Callie jumped down from the dumpster and blocked her escape. "Come on, Soriya. We took out a Tengu tonight. Challenge defeated. It's time to kick back and enjoy the night life."

"I can't. I have work," Urg said. He pointed to his watch and his eyes widened. "In ten minutes. And I smell like a damn monkey house."

Soriya smiled. She moved to pat his arm, then stopped. His sleeve was covered with a thick layer of mucus. She had no idea what animal might have left it. "I appreciate the assist."

"Any time, Soriya. But try to ask for help on my day off next time." Urg started for the street—and his obligation.

Callie called after him. "Hey, big guy. Where does an orc find work?"

Urg stopped at the mouth of the alley. "I'm a bouncer at Night Owls."

"The bar near Rogers?"

"That's the one," he said.

Callie grabbed Soriya's arm and pulled her toward the lumbering orc. "That's so funny! I was just on my way there myself. Come on."

Urg held them up. He pointed to Soriya. "She's fifteen."

"Sixteen," she said defiantly. Her cheeks flushed at the comment. She hated the way it made her feel. It wasn't like she was a child anymore. Or maybe her frustration was because of the freedom exuding from the woman she had just met, like there was nothing holding Callie back—nothing keeping her from enjoying life while also helping others. If it was all about balance, shouldn't Soriya be able to find some in her own life? Or would the Greystone always win out?

"Tomorrow," Urg clarified.

Her birthday. It hadn't come up in conversation much, but it was always in the back of her mind. Sixteen years old. It felt important somehow. Everything had of late.

Callie stepped between them. "It'll be fun." She tugged at Soriya and led her to the sidewalk. "How about some fun for once in your life?"

Her exuberance made Soriya grin. There was an energy in Callie that infected those around her. "Sure."

"Soriya?" Urg asked, wary of her choice.

"I'll be good, Urg," she said. "I promise."

Callie tilted her head down the block and gave the orc a wide berth. "Lead the way, big guy."

CHAPTER SIX

Shiva ran a finger across his skin. He poked his cheek and then his forehead. He stomped his naked feet against the ground. Every sensation brought a smile to his face.

He was *in* the world. Somehow, a door had opened to the other side, to the peace and heavenly tranquility of the Svarga Loka. There had been no question in his mind when it came to stepping through the green light. This was his time, and this was where his path had led him.

It was why he had carried the blade for so long. Shiva felt the pulsating darkness from the cold steel strapped to his back. It energized him and prodded him forward for his task.

Shiva had always known his path, always recognized the end of the story. However, until he'd reached the world, until he'd stepped onto the dock, he had never realized the necessity behind it all. Understanding came quickly.

The world was dank and frigid. His bare chest didn't help matters, but he suffered through it. Lights flashed and noise boomed through the streets of downtown. The city was a living, breathing organism long past its prime. It was in decay, full of filth, and lost in its way.

The homeless cowered in alleyways. They bundled against the cold, holding layers upon layers of discarded rags to keep warm. They muttered obscenities under their breath.

The streets should have been teeming with people. Instead, they were almost completely vacant. Lights flickered from apartments and in businesses. All were separate from each other, and all followed their own path rather than the spirit of community.

Shiva saw through them all. He witnessed the dregs of humanity lost in their ways, even through closed doors and shuttered windows. The lazy, the negligent, the abusive, and the vindictive. He saw no love or appreciation for the world as it was, only how far mankind had fallen over the centuries. He had been right to come. It was time for a change, to make the world a better place for all who deserved it.

And remove the rest from her care.

His walk carried him south, away from the spires of the city. Warehouses took over, and the desolation became more apparent with each block passed. Detritus flew in the wind. The residential areas were dotted with broken homes and boarded-up windows. They had been abandoned like the lives once held within. Humanity had been given so much, there was so much hope offered to them, yet all had been wasted on selfish need, on desire, and even more on hate.

At one corner, Shiva noticed two people huddled close together. One offered some paper, which was swiftly pocketed by the other. In return, the former was gifted with a small baggie containing white powder at the bottom. The sword along Shiva's back tingled with anticipation.

The addict, clutching tight to his score, blew past Shiva without a glance. Shiva hesitated for just a moment before continuing to the dealer. The man was short and thin, with dark skin and a ball cap on his head. He played with the paper, counting each one as if it meant the world to him.

Before Shiva could reach him, a hand blocked his path.

"Hold it," the figure said. He stood a foot taller than his companion. Despite the cold he wore a sleeveless shirt, likely to show off his musculature. A gold chain hung from his neck and a weapon poked out from the waistband of his sweatpants. "You look lost, son."

"I am not the one that is lost," Shiva remarked.

The guard eyed him over, curiously. "You sure you're in the right place?"

Shiva smiled. "Positive."

The short man joined them. "What'll it be, then?"

The guard held his companion back for a moment. "T, I don't like this. Something about this guy—"

"A paying customer, my brother," T said. "And we *always* treat our customers with respect."

"How can I do any less?" Shiva agreed with a slight bow. He pulled out the currency he had taken from the dead on the docks. It was crumpled and misshapen, but it caught their attention.

T's eyes grew wide. "What's your pleasure? I got the best in stock. All premium and all pure."

"Premium? Very likely," Shiva said. "Pure? Not since the womb, I'd imagine."

Shiva reached out and grabbed T. He pulled the dealer close, inspected him, and then took in a whiff of the man's odor. T tried to pry himself free, to no avail. "Hey!"

"T!" the guard cried. He fumbled for his gun, his hands shaking. "Let him go."

"Gladly." Shiva dropped the dealer to the ground. He unsheathed the blade along his back and stabbed T through the chest. The man's scream filled the air for a second, then silence returned.

The guard pointed his gun at Shiva. His eyes grew wide from the sight of the dead man at his feet. "You... You just... He was... and you... You killed him."

Shiva retrieved his sword, then stepped over the dead. He helped the guard lower his weapon. "If it makes you feel any better, you will see him soon. Along with so many others of your kind."

"My kind?"

"Sinners."

"Me?" the guard said and his voice quivered in fear. "No. I never done nothing like that. I never... Please, I..."

"Begging will avail you nothing. Your fate is set," Shiva said. The gun fell to the ground and the guard cowered before Shiva's blade. "However, there is one thing I need from you. Tell me and I will make your end quick."

"What?" the guard asked.

"Where can I find more like you?"

"Sinners?"

"Oh yes," Shiva answered excitedly. "I have *so* much more work to complete this night. This world requires saving and I intend to play my part in her rebirth."

CHAPTER SEVEN

The place was crowded, though Soriya didn't know why that surprised her. Most of her nights were spent wandering the streets, looking for trouble. She never stopped at a place, never sat back and watched the world take hold for any actual amount of time. There was only her job.

Portents held an unspoken rule: the night belonged to no one. Most listened. When the sun set, and when the red lights of the black tower at the heart of downtown washed over the city, it was mostly deserted.

Night Owls, however, was bursting with life. People stood in clumps against the bar. A constant flow of alcohol passed between patrons. Strangers danced in the corner by the jukebox, laughing and singing along. The tables were almost all taken. Stories were shared between friends or lovers.

Soriya and Callie sat at a small table opposite the bar. Soriya nursed her ice water, a straw sticking out of the glass. Two beers rested in front of Callie. She lifted one and took a swig. A satisfied look crossed her face when she set the bottle back down.

"Now *this* is living."

Soriya wasn't so sure. She knew the risk to each and every soul in the place. Portents wasn't safe at night. There was a reason for the rules, unspoken or not. Terror hid in the shadows, and it was her job to take that terror out before someone else got hurt. But those in Night Owls weren't rebels or troublemakers. To Soriya, they seemed almost desperate. Desperate to live. Desperate to love. Desperate for meaning.

"If you say so," she muttered as she played with her straw.

Callie clinked Soriya's glass with her beer. "Cheers."

Callie finished her first one and started in on the second. Soriya was amazed by the woman. She knew about the city and thrived in it. Nothing appeared to faze her. "So is this what you do for fun?"

"Among other things," Callie replied. "Life is too short, Soriya. Carpe diem and all that shit." Callie took another swig. The bottle returned to the table and she let out a long burp. She pounded her chest to get the last remnants out. "What about you? I want to hear what makes a kid like you want to hunt down the bad things in the night."

"Not a kid," Soriya said, too quickly and too sharply. "I'll be sixteen." She glanced at the clock hanging over the bar. The midnight hour had just begun. "Actually, looks like I am sixteen."

Callie lifted her bottle. "Happy birthday." She cheered at the new song that blasted from the jukebox. Her hips swayed in rhythm, lost in the revelry. Those that passed her offered a smile and a wave. None called her by name though. None stopped for more than a passing greeting. It didn't curb her enjoyment.

When she quieted for a second, Soriya leaned closer. "It's my job."

"What?" Callie shouted over the music.

"The hunting-down-monsters thing?" Soriya said, shifting by her side. "It's my job. My responsibility. My fate, really."

The smile faded from Callie's face. "Ah," she said, her tone serious and cold. "A girl with a destiny. I had a feeling. You had that look about you. Girl locked on one path is more like it."

"What do you mean?"

"Exactly that," Callie said. Her finger prodded Soriya in the chest. "You're so focused on one thing. Albeit, it's a damn important thing—to you at least. Still, you're letting the world pass you by."

"This is what I wanted," Soriya said. Mentor, her teacher, had given her a home and a place to study. Before that, she had known only loneliness in the orphanage. Mentor had shown her purpose, something to work toward. The Greystone was the protector of Portents. She stood against every darkness, every menace that made its way into the city. It was all she had ever wanted.

"You're sixteen," Callie said. Irritation crept into her voice. "How do you even know what you want in life?"

"I—"

"Soriya," Callie continued, not caring to stop. "You're a kid, for crying out loud. Maybe you really would've loved music or dance or friggin' chemistry. What if there was an option you never tried and *that* was what you were meant for in this life? Have you thought about that? Have you *really* experienced life?"

Soriya fell silent, unsure how to respond. She had only been five when Mentor saved her from Saint Helena's and the torture of the other girls. For the last decade she had studied under him, learned everything about the world through him, while housed in a small bunker buried beneath the city.

What *had* she seen in Portents? What had she actually experienced outside of what Mentor allowed for her? It would never compare to Callie, the connections, or the delight that seemed to follow the woman's every step.

Maybe there *was* something else for Soriya, a different path than the only one she had ever known. She had never had the dreams of a child with visions of becoming an astronaut, the president, or even something as mundane as a teacher.

Was Callie right?

Her newfound companion read her hesitation and a smug grin grew on her face. She patted Soriya's shoulder lightly. "Don't get bogged down on fate and destiny. Your life is your own. All I'm saying."

She picked up her two empties and started for the bar. Soriya called after her, "What are you doing?"

"Night's still young," Callie said. "I need a refill."

"Right. Of course."

"Water still good?" Callie asked.

Soriya glanced at the almost-full glass. She contemplated a different order, something new and exciting to her. Then she nodded. "Yeah. I'm good. Thanks."

"Sure, kid."

Callie made her way to the bar. She shifted between patrons

without issue. They let her through as if she was one of them, like she belonged in the world. Soriya wasn't sure she felt the same. She had spent so long underground, locked away with her endless lessons and drills while she tried to become the best warrior she could. To help others. It was an admirable goal— one she'd taken pride in all her life.

But seeing the woman before her, seeing Callie loving life gave Soriya the first inklings of doubt. How much better would Soriya's childhood have been in a normal setting? Away from the true city, away from the shadows? How much fun could Soriya have had, then?

It wasn't that simple. Nothing ever truly was. Callie topped the list at the moment. As she waited for her beers, the brazen woman leaned along the bar. Her eyes flitted to the door, then across the swath of humanity at Night Owls. She scanned the crowd, every member in turn, before moving to the next. All in seconds, yet Soriya caught it all as if it were in slow motion. Callie was searching for something—for someone.

Whoever it was made her nervous. Try as she might to hide it, they frightened Callie to no end.

CHAPTER EIGHT

This was a mistake. Callie stood at the bar, waiting impatiently for her drinks. Her nails tapped along the wood. She scanned the room back and forth. Satisfied when no one caught her eye, she returned to the the mirror behind the bar.

Soriya sat across the way. She sipped her water. The drink selection was the perfect representation of the girl: pure and innocent. Callie had thought her different when they'd met. It was in the smirk Soriya had held when she faced the Tengu, a rebellious attitude in the face of certain death. There was a strength in Soriya Greystone that had given Callie hope. Talking with her, however, revealed the truth.

Soriya was a kid. Her youth appeared to create a false front of impetuousness. Callie had believed it to be Soriya's strength. The truth of the matter, however, was that Soriya was too raw and too weakened by her role to understand the reality of the world. To see her struggle to answer Callie's questions made it all the more clear.

The girl wasn't up for facing Shiva. Callie had hoped differently when she'd intervened at the animal shelter. She had thought Soriya might have been the answer to her problems, a way to stop Shiva rather than face him directly.

She knew better now. Part of her was glad for the revelation. She liked Soriya, despite the weakness and the doubt. She saw herself in the teen's reckless abandon and her perseverance. Sending her against Shiva was a fool's errand, one that could only end one way. Callie needed a different solution, a better way, but none jumped out at her. Instead, she thanked the bartender for the pair of drinks and decided to let the night be the same as it ever was for Callie—pure joy.

She slid a ten-dollar bill across the bar for the beers. The bartender passed it back with an additional note on top containing his phone number. Callie tucked both in her bra and grinned mischievously at him. Then she started back to the table.

"I think he likes me," she proclaimed upon arriving. Soriya clearly was confused and Callie tilted her head to the bar. The young man behind the counter stared hungrily after them. Soriya's gaze returned to the table and her water.

"I'm sure you get that a lot," she remarked in a quiet tone. It made Callie grin: her naïveté at life. If Soriya showed a little skin and talked a little less about responsibility or fate, the world would open up for her.

"It's never enough," Callie said. She took a swig of her beer before lowering the bottle to the table. She soaked in the energy of the bar, and especially the crowd on their feet at the latest song. There was a complete disregard for the outside world. Shiva was in Portents, yet they were clueless how close their lives dangled on the precipice, how everything could fall and shatter like glass.

Soriya stared at her, drawing her back to the table.

"What?" Callie swiped at her nose and wiped at her lips. "What is it?"

"Ready to tell me what this is really all about?"

"I don't—"

Soriya stood up straight, fists at her side. "Not that I don't appreciate the diversion, but it's not every day a goddess of death pays me a visit."

Callie's mouth sat agape. Soriya had known the truth. Ignorant and naïve might not have been the best description for the teen after all. The woman who went by Callie recovered with a disarming smile. "What tipped you off?"

Soriya's eyebrow cocked. "Callie? Really?"

"Too on the nose?"

She nodded, then leaned against the table. "What do you want, *Kali*?"

"Can't a girl just want to have fun?" Kali answered. It was a lie. Her agenda was something completely different, but after meeting Soriya—after talking with her and spending the last hour by her side—she'd hoped for something more. It was why she planted the doubt in her eyes, why she continued to press the issue. She liked Soriya and wanted her to experience life as more than just an exercise in destiny. "I was hoping to show a budding stone bearer there can be more to life than blood and tears in this world. I *did* save you, Soriya. You could at least try and enjoy yourself."

"I am."

Kali shook her head. "No, you're not. You're trying to gauge me on a threat-level basis. Trying to find the danger in the room."

"So are you," Soriya shot back. "I saw you at the bar."

"I wasn't—"

"What are you running from, Kali?"

Kali chuckled nervously. She lifted her beer to her lips then set it back down. "Same thing as everyone else, Soriya. Everyone except you, apparently." She peered past Soriya, unable to look her in the eyes. A young man chatted with Urg at the front door. Car keys dangled from his fingers, though his attention was more focused on the woman with the tight red skirt at his side. He dropped the keys into his right pocket. Kali grabbed Soriya's arm and started for the exit. "Come on."

"What?" Soriya asked, a look of surprise on her face at the beverages left on the table. "Where?"

"To *live*, Soriya," Kali said. "To savor another night in this city."

Kali led them quickly for the door, just as the young man and his date entered. Kali collided with the new arrival, who nearly crashed into a table. Her fingers snatched the keys from his pocket and tucked them away.

"I'm so sorry!" Kali exclaimed in a high-pitch voice. The young man patted his shirt awkwardly, though his full attention was on Kali's exposed cleavage. "I am *such* a klutz tonight."

"My fault," he replied. "Really."

His date cleared her throat and he retreated sheepishly to her side. Kali waved, then moved for the exit with Soriya close behind.

"What was that all about?"

Kali shrugged. "I tripped."

"Right," Soriya muttered.

The night air was cool. The wind picked up in the late hour. Before they could fully experience the temperature shift, a hand blocked their escape.

"Hold it," Urg said. He rose from his stool by the door and filled the frame with his massive bulk. "Don't think I didn't see that, lady."

"Lady?" Kali scoffed. "Listen, big guy, you've had it out for me since—"

"You took that man's—"

"Don't even think of accusing me of anything," Kali snapped back. She pulled Soriya forward. "We both know this is about you not trusting Soriya to do the right thing."

"What?" Urg exclaimed. "That's not... I..."

"It's okay, Urg," Soriya said. "I'm fine."

"Yeah," Kali said, with a wink. "Let her be her own person."

Urg settled back to allow them to leave. He stopped Soriya with a gentle touch against her arm. "Be careful."

"I will."

Kali separated them, taking Soriya's hand. "How about we don't tonight?"

She laughed and the two started down the block. Urg clearly didn't trust Kali and his concern was justified. What she had originally intended for Soriya was left behind and there was only a night free from burden and responsibility before them. Kali wanted nothing more than to forget about Shiva and whatever nightmare he had brought with him to the city.

Kali removed the keys from her pocket and hit the unlock button repeatedly until a car blinked in response. It sat at the end of the block: a sharp red Mustang.

"What are you doing?" Soriya asked in confusion. She looked over the car. "Wait, is this yours?"

"Right now?" Kali said with a giggle. She tossed the keys over to Soriya. "It's yours."

Soriya caught them, eyes wide. "What do you mean?"

Kali pulled her close. "It's your sixteenth birthday, right? I think it's time for your first driving lesson."

CHAPTER NINE

Alejo Ruiz couldn't sleep. It had been the same all week. He'd waited until his wife had fallen asleep, flipping through pages of his book, though he had no idea what was actually on the written page thanks to his bleary eyes. Once he was satisfied she was out like a light, Ruiz attempted to join her in slumber.

Her discomfort always woke her quickly. It had come within minutes of him sidling up to her under the sheets. Once the first movement hit, the second soon followed, and by then he had already surrendered to another sleepless night.

He'd tried the couch as an alternative. The sunken cushions usually served as a nice respite during weekend afternoons. At night, however, it never lasted. There had been the clock to move from the room. Its ticking boomed as soon as the lights went out. On top of that was the clicking of the furnace; it was most likely on its last legs, though Ruiz refused to have it serviced so late in the season. That was next winter's problem.

Forty-five minutes into his latest bout of insomnia, Ruiz gave up. He threw off the thin blanket—the only one he had been able to find in the dark—and stumbled through the darkened home in search of his shirt and tie. They were still in the basement awaiting the iron, but they were clean enough to pass for a quick trip out.

Work would make things right. It would settle his nerves and bring him rest. Ruiz had put it off all week. There were discussions about heading to the Central Precinct, his home away from home for his entire law-enforcement career, but he had surrendered to the needs of his family. They came first, or so he tried to believe.

Leaving the couch behind, Ruiz crept down the hall. He slipped past his bedroom, where Michelle still tossed and turned between heavy breaths. He stopped at the next doorway.

His daughters slept soundly. Teresa, now six, still managed to move in every direction while she slept. Zoe, his oldest at twelve, muffled her sister's snoring with an extra pillow over her head.

Ruiz lived for them. They made his time at work palatable. Everything he had done in his life was for their benefit, yet work continued to pull at him. The precinct demanded more time, more commitment. He had sworn it was for them, the sleeping angels he had been given to care for, but lately it didn't seem to be enough.

There was always another case to crack or a murder to solve. It tore at him, the need to keep his family safe over the desire to spend every waking moment with them. He did everything for them, but when he didn't see them and couldn't be with them, was he really adding anything of value to their lives or simply depriving them of their father?

It was a question that had haunted his sleep all week. It carried him from his children's shared room to the small bedroom at the end of the narrow corridor. The nursery. He had spent weeks working on it—weeks away from the office. The baby could come at any moment, but so far there was quiet and emptiness in the room.

Ruiz still had trouble wrapping his head around the idea of another child. Was it the wrong choice? Had he been wrong to have faith things could get better? Ruiz wished for answers and found only the silence of the night filling his home.

He needed to go out and do some work. He started for the kitchen as his fingers fiddled with his tie. The knot tightened around his neck, and he straightened the thin silk so it lay along the buttons of his shirt. Ruiz collected his keys from the hook by the back door. As he reached for the handle, a low creak escaped from the floorboards. Not his own, but from behind him.

"Sneaking out, Captain Ruiz?" The light clicked on. Ruiz shielded his eyes from the brightness. He slowly turned to face his accuser.

Michelle looked stunning despite the late hour. She leaned against the side of the door frame, one hand near the light and the other over her extended belly. She rubbed at the life inside her. It seemed to have a calming effect on Michelle, and he was grateful for her restraint. It failed to dim the fire in her eyes though.

"Michelle—"

"Nuh-uh," she replied. "Pregnant women go first. There has to be a law about that written somewhere."

Ruiz smiled. "Only on the back of my eyelids."

His joke did nothing to win her over. She shuffled deeper into the room and he met her near the table. She took the keys dangling from his hands.

"Alejo, we talked about this."

It was the reason he was home in the first place. *The talk.* He had missed the births of both Zoe and Teresa. He had been at the hospital in the aftermath, but the actual birth had been witnessed only by Michelle's sister and the staff of the maternity ward. Work had won out for both occasions, and she had accepted it at the time. Not this time, however. Now, he had been asked to walk away from his demanding job for the last month to witness the miracle of birth.

He had accepted wholeheartedly. Not being there for his wife in her time of need had become one of his greatest regrets. But, he was on edge—cut off from the world he had been immersed in for the lion's share of each day. It was like he had lost a limb, yet still felt it with every movement.

"Yes," Ruiz admitted. "We did talk about it."

"Yet, you're leaving me," Michelle said. She squeezed his hands tighter. "When I'm like this. A beached whale."

"A beautiful one."

She dropped his hands and scoffed. "So I *am* a whale."

Ruiz shook his head, hands to his hips. "I walked right into that one."

"I need you here, Alejo," Michelle said. She pulled out a chair and sat down. Her hand ran the length of her belly. There was concern in her eyes, but more than that, there was disappointment. He hated that look. It had become the norm for her over the years. "Let someone else handle things at the precinct. I need… this baby needs you here."

He knelt at her side, joining her hand along her stomach. "And I will be here when it is time."

"I've heard that one before."

"I've earned that, I have. I've disappointed you in the past. But I've been here for you and will continue to be here for you. Always."

"Just not right now," she muttered.

Ruiz sighed, then stood. He took the keys in hand. "There are reports, Michelle. Cases I oversaw that need my approval, so I can make sure the proper warrants are issued. I planned to head in at some point this week to take care of them, but since I couldn't sleep I thought I would—"

"Right," she said, clearly not caring for the explanation.

"It's important, hon," Ruiz said.

Michelle's hands clasped the sides of her belly. "*This* is supposed to be important. You promised to make this the priority."

"I will," Ruiz said. He pointed to the clock. It was minutes after midnight. "I'll only be gone a few hours. You get some sleep."

"Like this? Not a chance."

Ruiz leaned down and kissed his wife's forehead. "Try."

She attempted to hold him in place, forcing a kiss on the lips. Her frustration was clear, but a fight wasn't the answer. It never had been for them. She knew the job and what it required. She also knew whom she had married.

Still, she kept him close. Her brilliant brown eyes shone in the light of the kitchen. "I need this kid out of me, Alejo. And I need you there for it."

Ruiz nodded. "I will be there." He read her thin glare clearly. "I will, Michelle."

He moved for the door, but she stopped him at the knob. "This was supposed to be our time. This was supposed to be perfect."

A sad smile escaped him as he opened the door. "Get some sleep. I'll be back before breakfast. Everything *will* be perfect. I promise."

She said nothing as he left. Her shadow followed him to the car, but it never deterred him. He only needed a few hours to finish some work. Then he could rest. Then he could focus on his family. *Just a few hours.*

His promise felt hollow as the light clicked off in the home and he pulled out of the driveway.

CHAPTER TEN

Soriya fought to keep her eyes open. The struggle came not out of exhaustion from the long night, but from a growing fear, one she had never known before.

A fear of driving.

She could barely control the Mustang. Her hands clenched tightly to the steering wheel, and her foot hardly touched the gas pedal, yet the car zoomed down the almost vacant streets like a bullet from a gun.

From Night Owls they had gone south toward Heaven's Gate Park. Nothing felt natural behind the wheel of the car. Every shift was nerve-wracking; each twist in the road caused the car to swerve rather than glide naturally. The tightly winding streets of downtown, with parked cars lining the blocks at all hours, did nothing but make her more tense. The more tension that ran through her body, the worse the jostling of the car— both in terms of speed and direction.

Soriya had never hated anything more in her entire life. She would have preferred to face a *thousand* Tengus than operate a motor vehicle.

The expressway was meant to offer relief. Open road and little traffic would give her a chance to get comfortable at the skill. She was sixteen. Driving was supposed to be natural when one came of age, a progression into adulthood. It was a skill, and she had been diligent in learning everything Mentor had offered. This one was no different, yet felt completely wrong at the same time.

The RDJ, the massive eight-lane highway that wound

through the city of Portents like a snake, was closed. She had forgotten to take that into account. Major construction was being done in no less than three sections of the heavily traveled artery, forcing massive congestion everywhere else in the city.

The ramp was blocked by multiple barricades, the ROAD CLOSED sign reflecting off her headlamps. Since she was so focused on the obstacle, Soriya failed to glance up at the red light hovering over the next intersection. A car skirted through and made a left-hand turn directly in front of her.

"Car, car, car!" she yelled. Her foot slammed on the brake, but the Mustang continued to rush ahead. The driver of the car in the intersection honked his horn while completing his turn a second before Soriya would have hit him.

Kali howled from the passenger seat. Her window was rolled down and her hair blew free in the frigid wind. Soriya wanted to scream at the other woman. She wanted to stop the car, walk away, and forget she'd ever met the lunatic at her side. But there was something in Kali's laugh, something in her lust for life, that Soriya found compelling.

"Soriya!" Kali shouted, snapping her attention back to the road. "Might want to do something."

They were still heading for the barrier. She had let go of the brake accidentally and their momentum carried them forward.

"Oh, hell," Soriya whispered.

Kali grabbed the wheel and pulled hard. "Right! Turn right!"

Tires screeched at the sudden shift in direction. The car bumped up and down from her uneven pace on the accelerator. The Mustang hopped the curb before returning to the right side of the road. Soriya glanced back, almost afraid at what damage might have been caused during her wide turn. When she looked ahead she found herself under another red light—another mistake in a long night of them. Kali continued to howl with laughter. She roared and clapped with each disaster.

"How can you be enjoying this?" Soriya asked.

"How can you not?"

Soriya tightened her grip on the wheel. She tried to catch her breath, tried to calm her body, but the tension built up with each block passed. Eventually, she let up on the accelerator.

"I'm going to pull over."

Kali shook her head. "I wouldn't."

Her passenger adjusted the rearview mirror. Flashing lights beamed from behind them. The sound of a siren cut through the pounding of Soriya's heart in her chest. "Oh, no."

"Oh, yes," Kali said. "Probably for the reckless driving. Could be the stolen car though."

"*Stolen?*"

"Borrowed," Kali clarified. She shrugged her shoulders. "They always confuse those two."

A stolen car. How had she not realized? What the hell had she been thinking going on a jaunt with Kali? If Mentor found out... No, *when* Mentor found out, it would be the end for her. There would be no more training—no more Greystone.

Was that the lesson Kali wanted to impart? Her talk about fighting fate, of walking different paths, stuck with Soriya. Had she forced Soriya into a bad decision knowing what it might cost her in the end?

"Hey, kid," Kali called. "Might want to turn the wheel."

The intersection ahead was blocked. A tractor-trailer was backing up to make a delivery. There were too many obstacles on the road, too many life-threatening situations everywhere she turned. The sirens continued to blare behind her.

Tires squealed as she spun the wheel right once more. The Mustang turned, but not quickly enough, and it bounced off the side of the truck as it completed the turn. Soriya threw an awkward wave as they left the intersection and the screaming driver behind.

"Sorry!" she exclaimed. "I'm really sorry!"

The police continued their pursuit. Soriya eased off the gas and her hands left the steering wheel.

"We can explain this, Kali," she said. "I'll just pull over and talk it out with them."

"Or—" Kali lifted her leg and slammed her foot down over Soriya's on the accelerator. "—we could not."

"What are you doing?" Soriya bellowed over the sound of Kali's manic laugh. The Mustang shot ahead and Soriya clenched the wheel for dear life, wishing she could close her eyes and make it all disappear. "Kali!"

CHAPTER ELEVEN

The bodyguard had been wise not to lie to Shiva. He had spouted a number of locations before his death. None had interested Shiva as much as the establishment on a street called Salem.

It was a temple, though the moniker no longer held any meaning—at least to those outside its walls. Within, however, was a different story completely, with its inhabitants worshiping foul deeds performed night and day.

Shiva stopped short to marvel at the architecture. He had never stood before the grandeur of a Hindu temple. While the sheen had been lost over time, the statues positioned outside remained intact. They oversaw the entire street, gazing down on any passing pedestrian like gods among men. They were guardians to the treasures within, those once of the soul and now only of the flesh.

It had become a drug den. The house of worship had once been a place to sow the seeds of redemption through sacrifice and prayer. Now, however, it only brought them to their knees in revulsion. Sin overtook the meaning behind the place, and the sinners thrived inside.

Shiva stepped up to the large archway which provided entry into the temple. The smell hit him first: decay and rot. Sanitation did not appear to be a concern, though it was desperately needed in the poorly ventilated sanctuary.

Pillars ran along the side of the walls. Between them, the walls contained the figureheads of his faith—or *murti* as they came to be called. Brahma and Vishnu oversaw the entryway.

They guarded against the evil of the world. They failed, just as they always had.

Their passive nature had allowed this to happen, and their faith in humanity had led them astray. They had been confident in the belief that all would be forgiven in the end. They had become self-involved and repugnant, so swept up in the flesh they had forgotten the spirit.

There were almost a dozen people in the mandapa. They barely noted Shiva's arrival; they were lost in their own drug-addled states. They shot up and drank, they danced and screamed. All the while, they were unaware of the world around them or the end to come.

"Remarkable," Shiva said. He shifted between the dregs of the city, the ones who had slipped through the cracks of society and created a new one that suited them. They were gluttons and addicts, layabouts and castoffs, and they did nothing for others but wasted space.

Shiva had a purpose for them.

The blade across his back pulsed with anticipation. He had hidden it away for centuries. Its purpose had been lost to the ages, but it remained locked in his mind. It was his destiny, the one thing he had truly lived for, and now he finally had the opportunity to fulfill it. He could bring about the end of his story and the return of glory for the world.

He was so close. Shiva's body trembled from the thought. Since he was so caught up in the moment, in the sanctity of his holy temple, he failed to notice a newcomer to the room.

"Help you with something?" The man-child wore an oversized sweatshirt with jeans. His eyes were bloodshot and he wiped at his nose every few seconds. His body swayed as if listening to music. Shiva wondered if he might simply fall at the passing of a breeze.

Shiva continued through the heart of the temple to the altar on the far end. "You already have. Your capacity for depravity astounds me. Tell me, why do they do it?"

"Who?"

Shiva pointed at the outcasts at the man's feet. They rolled around, moaning with each hit; their eyes were glazed over from the conversation happening in front of them. "Why do they poison themselves to the brink of death?"

The man sniffed, then pulled at his nose. His hands shook with each movement. "How else do you know you're alive?"

Shiva nodded. He had heard the excuse over the millennia. "And you sell this to them?" Shiva asked. "This escape from reality?"

"We all need one," the man said. "That's why you're here, isn't it? Only reason someone like you would come here in the first place."

"Someone like me," Shiva muttered. He returned to the altar in the small chamber known as the antarala. More statues dominated the space: the deities he had served with, and the figureheads that had done nothing but watch from the void of their heavenly space. Above the altar, though, sat his own image. It stared at him, hands reaching out to envelop those beneath and swallow the world whole. "You don't know how right you are."

"Yo!" someone shouted from the back of the temple. He raced out from the back, a gun in his hand. "Who this?"

The man-child in the hooded sweatshirt shrugged. "Didn't catch a name, Felix."

Felix stuck his pistol in Shiva's face. "This ain't a convenience store, bro. How'd you find us?"

"I never learned his name. He worked for someone called T. He told me of this place," Shiva said. He unsheathed the demon blade, letting the obsidian steel glint under the dim lights. "Right before I killed him."

"You..." Felix's hand shook as he gripped the gun. "You what?"

Shiva stepped forward, letting the barrel press against his brow. "I offered him my services and he gratefully accepted. As you will now."

"You... You're damn crazy to think that," Felix said. He stepped away. There was terror in his eyes. The gun remained locked on the target, but his finger wavered along the trigger. "Yo!"

Footsteps rushed into the room from all directions. A dozen men entered, all armed and ready for a fight. Confusion followed. None of them were sure of the man with the bare chest and sword. They only seemed to know how to follow orders— to kill those who stood in the way of their small corner of the world.

Shiva laughed. It echoed in the open space of the temple and filled the corridors. The sound snapped the addicts on the floor from their delirious highs, and brought all their attention back to him.

"So we do understand each other," Shiva bellowed for all to hear. He pointed his blade toward Felix. "I thank you for your assistance."

"What the hell are you—?"

Felix never finished the sentence. He didn't flinch, didn't react at all. Shiva was too fast. The god of destruction's blade thrust ahead and skewered the drug dealer. Blood filled the man's mouth and dribbled from his lips. Shiva removed the blade, the black pulsing brighter along the steel. Felix fell before him. The others in the room stared silently.

Shiva turned to them, white eyes burning for more. He raised his sword toward the sinners and smiled. "Feel free to scream now."

CHAPTER TWELVE

"She did *what?*"

Mentor attempted to hold back his anger. He paced the entrance to Night Owls. His knee ached, but he barely felt it over his rising anger.

Soriya was supposed to return home after finishing things with the Tengu. That had not gone as planned. Few things did with the teen, but to find out she had attended a bar, of all places, to celebrate her victory was only the icing on the cake of the story told by the looming orc.

"It wasn't—" Urg stopped at the sound of shouting on the corner. Both turned to see a man and his escort for the evening staring at the vacant spot on the street.

"My car!" the man cried. "I parked it right here!" He was wearing a navy blue suit jacket and khakis. He patted his pockets in a desperate search. "Where the hell are my keys?"

The escort, clearly not his wife judging by the pressed-on nails and tight red skirt, reached for his shoulder. "Baby, you need to calm—"

He pulled away in a rage. "Do *not* tell me to calm down!"

The woman huffed, then stomped back to the bar. She passed the watchful gaze of Mentor and Urg. There was a slight pause in her step and her nails grazed Urg's forearm. The orc cocked his head casually toward the dance floor and shut the door as soon as she entered. When the man returned to the club, Urg blocked the door.

"What the hell? Are you serious?"

"Always," Urg answered, arms across his chest. "I don't need you stirring up drama at my place."

"Great! Just great!" The man threw his hands into the air. He cursed the entire block before his words were lost to the wind.

Mentor took a deep breath, then cleared his throat. "Soriya did this?"

Urg relaxed at his post, his arms fell to his sides, and he leaned along the wall. "Not alone. And not exactly willingly. Sort of."

Mentor's jaw clenched. He was trying to rein in his fatherly tendencies. They had caused problems recently, especially during their time with the Minotaur. His concern for her safety and the choices she'd made had created a rift that almost tore them apart completely. Soriya had fought to mend their relationship and he could do no less.

Still, her need for connections vexed him. It always had. Friendships led to distractions from the work. They had a task to fulfill, and the utmost concentration was required at all times.

Urg was an exception to the rule for Mentor, though at the moment he regretted it. When they had met, Mentor viewed the orc as a kindred spirit of sorts. Urg had always stood as a protector of the child. He always did what he could to keep Soriya safe from harm at a young age. He also inspired her curiosity in the strangeness of their world.

Urg had been one of the few specials to leave the confines of the Courtyard, a metaphysical crossroads hidden in the city. Where most preferred only the occasional visit to Portents, Urg had decided to live in the city. He had found a job. He hid his unique origins in plain sight. His height and his green skin all played to the role he served at the bar as a bouncer. He had never strayed down a darker path as so many other myths and legends had once they found their way to Portents. Mentor admired that.

"Who was she with?" Mentor finally asked.

"Indian woman," Urg said. "She was a big drinker. Called herself—"

"Callie."

Urg's eyes blinked and he shook his head. "How could you possibly know that?"

Kali. After all these years...

Mentor grimaced. "I can't believe she still uses that ridiculous name. Although at this moment, I can't believe a lot of things."

"I didn't call you to blow Soriya in," Urg said. "She's a good kid."

"I know," Mentor replied. "This isn't Soriya's fault."

It was his. Kali was a name from the past, one he had kept from Soriya. It was yet another secret. They were piling up around him like firewood for a pyre. Each had the potential to set off a spark and burn everything he had built to the ground.

He had let Kali go after their last encounter. She had helped his investigation into a series of grisly murders, so he had given her a pass. At the time it had seemed to be the right call. Now, he regretted that decision.

"What are you going to do?" Urg asked.

"That is the question, isn't it?"

He wasn't sure how to address the situation. The last time Soriya slipped up he'd punished her severely. He had sidelined her against the Minotaur. She disobeyed, and her anger had almost torn their relationship asunder. Arguing wasn't the answer. He needed to understand her thoughts. She was going through too much too quickly. She was a teenager, after all. She was fifteen... No, sixteen now.

Her birthday had arrived without pomp and pageantry. He hadn't even acknowledged the upcoming event during their last conversation. He'd wanted to surprise her. Instead, after finding out Soriya's activities for the night, Mentor was the one surprised.

"I have to find them," Mentor said. "See what Soriya was—"

Sirens began to sound, drowning out his words. Patrol cars raced down the block. They headed for Lowtown. Not a stretch of the imagination, given the area. It was the number of cruisers involved that gave Mentor pause. More lights flashed up and down the street, all headed in a single direction.

"You think it's them?" Urg said. He tried to gauge Mentor's reaction to the police presence.

"No," Mentor said. He trailed the cruisers, then began to follow. "This is something else. Something much worse."

CHAPTER THIRTEEN

"This the car?"

The Mustang rested near the corner of Taylor and Hall. The passenger-side tires sat on the curb, and the front end was nestled against a mailbox, which tipped awkwardly forward. The engine was still running and the driver's-side door was open.

There had been no time for anything else. Soriya had sped ahead a few blocks, made some dangerous turns, and then brought the joyride to a grinding halt. Kali had resisted. For her, the fun of their escapade was clearly enough to justify a longer jaunt. Soriya, though, had already left the vehicle behind in a race to beat the cops' arrival. Reluctantly, Kali had followed.

They sat perched on the fire escape of a building diagonal from the car. Soriya let the shadows of the four-story complex swallow her up. Kali was more brazen, balancing along the ledge of the roof. Soriya kept watch over the scene.

Two officers approached—one male and one female. Both looked to be in their mid-thirties, though the woman was obviously the senior of the pair as she led the investigation of the stolen Mustang.

"That's what the report says," the woman said. Their voices carried across the intersection. "Did you see anyone run off as we approached?"

"Not a soul," the male officer replied. He glanced around, hand over his service weapon. "Who are we looking for exactly?"

"Two women," she answered. "They were young, at least as far as I could tell during the chase. Darker skin for both, possibly sisters. You know, the type of situation you're always on the prowl for."

"A guy's gotta dream," he said as he circled the car. He scanned the area and Soriya retreated along the fire escape, letting the shadows help hide her. The man eventually shrugged. "Looks like they're long gone."

"Perfect!" Kali laughed. Soriya jumped from her position. She grabbed hold of the ledge and flipped onto the roof. Kali clapped her hands, and the sound was even louder than her laughing. "That was perfect!"

Soriya grabbed Kali and led her away from the ledge. Flashlights beamed toward the fire escape, but the two women had shifted out of their path. Soriya continued to guide Kali behind a billboard overlooking the intersection.

Kali freed herself from Soriya's grip. "The wind in your hair. The power at your fingertips. It was exhilarating, wasn't it?"

"It was wrong, Kali," Soriya said. She paced the length of the rooftop. The flashlight beams grew brighter as the officers made a sweep of the area. They were getting closer and Kali was not helping. When Soriya returned, she leaned along the back of the billboard and kept her voice low. "I shouldn't have listened to you. Shouldn't have—"

"What? Shouldn't have had a little fun?" Kali said. She groaned then ran her hands over her face. She pointed to the beams of light, which slowly faded in the distance. "That's something they can't understand. Any of them. These people are so stuck in place, with their rules and regulations. What does that do except squash free will? People deserve to live while they can. Mortality doesn't give many second chances."

"You're wrong," Soriya snapped. She pushed off the billboard and crept toward the ledge. The cops were on their way back to their cruiser. The woman made one last stop at the Mustang, while she reported it back to the station over her radio. Soriya crouched along the edge of the rooftop. "It's not about squashing people or taking something away, Kali. It's about protecting them. That's why I do what I can."

Kali rolled her eyes. Her hands were on her hips. "Back to this, then. Your so-called destiny."

"It's... it's what I've always wanted," Soriya said. She bit her bottom lip, angry at her own hesitation. Being the Greystone, utilizing the mysterious stone to protect the city, had always been her goal. Over a decade of training had led her to taking the role from Mentor. This was her time now. It truly was what she wanted... wasn't it? Soriya shook the thought away. She stood and returned to the center of the rooftop. "I'm sorry you don't have that in your life."

"Don't be," the goddess replied, though her eyes fell to the ground at her words. "I never wanted anything more than I already have."

Joy, pure and unencumbered—that was Kali's life. Running from place to place, person to person, with no deep meaning behind it all. All Kali required was the pleasure of the moment before the next took hold. There was no depth, no purpose behind it, and that was the point. She seemed to want nothing more from those around her, nor from the city as a whole. It was merely her playground to use as she saw fit.

Yet, for some reason, she had come to Soriya's rescue. She had stopped the Tengu; she had diverted from her path of frivolity to save Soriya. *Why?* It didn't line up. Kali didn't appear to care about anyone, not really. They were simply placeholders who helped her find a laugh for a second. When the happiness faded she moved to the next.

Soriya had just reached that end. She could see it in Kali's slumped shoulders and her lowered gaze. Soriya had no more to offer Kali.

"This was fun, Kali," Soriya said. She stared out over the city, following the trail of the cruiser as it departed. "But I have to go."

Kali shook her head. She grabbed Soriya's shoulder and turned her away from the road. "Why? How can you be so naïve to it all?"

"How can *you?*"

Soriya pointed out over the city. Kali stepped up to the ledge for a closer look. The cruiser's lights were on and the siren cut through the silence. The officers raced out of the downtown area.

From their vantage point, the two women on the rooftop could see more flashing lights in the distance. There was one set four blocks over to the east and another to the west. All sped through Portents, and all were heading in the same direction.

Soriya jumped from the ledge to the fire escape. The metal clanged under her sneakers. She peered up at Kali, who wrapped her arms tight across her chest. Soriya held out a hand. "Coming with me? They might need some help."

"Not a chance," Kali said. She stepped into the shadows of the billboard. "Whatever it is… it has nothing to do with me."

Soriya nodded, then started for the street below. Kali's words stung. She had hoped in getting to know Kali that there was a chance she might have found a kindred spirit—someone who understood the city and was willing and able to fight to keep the beasts at bay.

As she reached the street, Soriya suddenly felt the cold of the city in a way she never had before. Worse, she realized how truly alone she was. There was another threat, another menace in the city. Maybe she wasn't needed, but part of her knew there would always be something else pulling at her and driving her forward. Another disaster to be averted, another killer that needed to be stopped.

The burden stacked upon her shoulders and she struggled to carry it as she ran after the speeding cruisers into the night. For a brief moment she envied Kali for the life she had chosen. It was truly a life free of all obligation and responsibility.

CHAPTER FOURTEEN

Kali stood in silence as she watched Soriya make her way down to the street. The teen ran after the wave of police cruisers heading toward the fading light in the distance. Kali knew what she would find there. It was the only thing ever left in Shiva's wake: the dying and the dead.

Soriya would understand that in time, hopefully before it was too late. Kali was surprised by the young woman's strength and her determination no matter the danger. It would take her far, yet it would also bring her nothing more than an ugly end. Soriya Greystone was certainly strong-willed, but foolish as hell.

Shiva could not be stopped. Kali had already witnessed the massacre at the docks. Nothing could stop him from attaining his every whim. He was an unstoppable force of destruction. And he hadn't come alone.

He had the demon blade with him. She thought the weapon had been lost to time, but she could feel the presence of the dreaded sword with each use—with each death that followed Shiva's path. He had come to change things, to make his mark on the world. He would not leave until the entire planet was scarred. He called it *transformation*. He believed it to be for the better.

Kali, however, knew the truth: his goal was nothing more than the end of everything. She wanted to run. Not into the fire with Soriya, but as far from it as possible. Kali had lived her life in the shadow of his presence. She had always feared the day of his arrival.

Fate had to be a lie. It had to be.

She had worked so long, fought so hard, to live a life free from doubt and worry. Kali's entire existence was perpetuated on the notion of free will, on the ability to walk away from the doom and gloom that pulled people from contentment more often than not. She needed that joy to fulfill and sustain her. Pleasure took away her fear; it decimated the need for connections and responsibilities. Most importantly, it kept her from her fate.

Soriya's shadow disappeared in the darkness of the city. She raced toward her destiny, to be the Greystone: a protector of others and a warrior-born.

Kali was anything but. However, as her newfound companion disappeared amid the spires in the distance, Kali hesitated. Soriya was heading toward destruction. She was in danger. Everyone was in danger now.

Even Kali's joyful little world.

Could Soriya truly stop Shiva? Was it possible for the young woman to stand up and defeat the unstoppable force?

Kali couldn't take the chance. Not now. Not ever. Facing Shiva meant reconciling her beliefs on fate. She wasn't willing to do that. Her life was her own. She deserved it. She earned her happiness. No one could tell her differently. No one could demand she step in front of that bullet.

Kali left the comfort of the rooftop ledge for the fire escape. The metal steps creaked under her as she made her way to the street. She started toward the flashing lights and the blaring sirens of the police cruisers in the distance.

Soriya was different than anyone she had ever met. If there was someone who might stand in the path of Shiva, it was the plucky teen with the Greystone. Had Soriya been the answer Kali had been looking for—a way to save the world and herself?

It was worth a shot.

She broke into a run, following the trail left by Soriya. Kali had to tell her the truth. She had to give the girl the best shot possible. For the sake of Portents and for herself.

Fate be damned.

CHAPTER FIFTEEN

Ruiz should have passed on the call. When the phone rang at his desk he had been closing up his first report of the night. He was already feeling drowsy from the work. His insomnia had been taken care of the moment he finalized the warrant necessary in a search-and-seizure case that had been held up thanks to improper documentation. It had been the exact thing he feared would happen due to his absence. All it took was one legal loophole for a criminal to sneak through, and he had given them plenty by prioritizing his family over his job.

That frustration had caused him to pick up the phone. The curses that followed after learning what had happened came from his inability to ever set aside his work. Michelle needed him. He had made a promise when the possibility of a third child was initially discussed—an honest desire to step up as a father and deliver this time. He had failed in the initial two outings, though Zoe and Teresa didn't hold it against him. He was a cop. The job was strenuous enough without having to be burdened by the expectations of others: his own were enough to handle.

He wanted to be there for his wife, wanted to commit to walking away from the office and the caseload, but the work hung over him. He truly *had* only come in to catch up on reports.

Until the call came in.

Ruiz had made his way to the temple in silence. He took his own car, not one of the dozen cruisers allocated to handle the scene. He'd needed the quiet of the road and the solitude of his own thoughts to carry him to another crime scene. There was another murderer in his city, another threat he had hoped would never come.

The call from the docks had been mentioned when he first arrived to the station. Six bodies were found stacked like kindling near the southside seaport. Detectives had been assigned and resources allocated to handle the scene. Ruiz put it out of his mind, hoping it had been an isolated incident. Instead, it appeared to be nothing more than a first strike.

He waved to the officer manning the cordon on the western block. The man nodded and let Ruiz drive through to park on the side street. While he exited his car, Ruiz stared at the chaos of the night in Portents.

Murder and mayhem.

That was how Detective Greg Loren always described it. For a second, Ruiz wished Loren had been by his side. Murder of this degree—a slaughter from what was passed along during the call—required his best detective. But Loren was away on his honeymoon. His priority was his newly-minted bride.

Ruiz sighed. He shuffled his feet along the road for the temple. Loren deserved the break. He had pushed it off for months following the wedding in order to close his caseload to the best of his ability. It surprised Ruiz how much he had come to trust in the man, and how Loren's friendship mattered more than his clearance rate. He had never been one to grow close to his colleagues. He'd preferred to focus on the work and his home life.

It was funny how much things had changed over the years.

But not Portents. No, the city continued on the same course it had for decades. Crime didn't just spike: it grew like a disease. It festered in the quiet corners, like in the temple he must have passed a thousand times before and never noticed.

A towering officer watched over the front door. His hat was askew on his head and a dopey grin spread along his lips. John Pratchett belonged more to a 1950's Mayberry-esque department than the current regime, but he was always present, serving as a regular guardian at the gate.

"Captain?" he asked as Ruiz approached.

Ruiz nodded to the man before slipping inside. "Pratchett."

Pratchett followed at his back, nipping at his heels. "I thought you were on leave? Did the baby—?"

Ruiz stopped and held up a hand. "Take a breath, Pratchett. I came in for some reports, and then this hit the airwaves. What have we got so far?"

"A busy night," Pratchett replied. "You heard about the docks?"

"Unfortunately." Ruiz shifted out from under the gateway to the temple and into the first room. His phone slipped into his hand and he tapped the screen. No missed calls and no messages waited for him from his wife. He had checked not five minutes earlier, and would no doubt do so again.

His promise dogged him at every turn. He should have stayed home with her and helped her fall back asleep. He should have let the work go for his family's sake. Instead, he added to the great divide that had split them apart for so long: the secrets and lies he had created thanks to the true nature of the city.

"Mitchell and Davis have this one, sir," Pratchett said. There was concern in his eyes over the silence that had fallen and the presence of the phone in Ruiz's hand. "You don't have to—"

The captain tucked the phone back into his pocket. "Show me."

Pratchett led the way deeper into the temple. They didn't have to go far. Above them, light poured through a series of windows decorating the ceiling. It cast a heavenly glow over everything, yet did little to take away the horror Ruiz found waiting for him. Bodies were strewn about the main hall. They lay over furniture and in piles on the floor. Most clutched tight to weapons, which apparently hadn't helped save them from the slaughter.

"It's the same M.O. as the other scene," Pratchett said.

"Was this guy in a hurry or something?" Ruiz commented as he scanned the scene. Forensics handled the room professionally. Photographers snapped images of every inch of the room, while specialists pulled shell casings from the walls and the floorboards. Everything was cataloged; every shred of possible evidence was saved for analysis back at the precinct.

Ruiz stopped near one of the victims. He crouched low and

carefully slipped on a pair of gloves. Silently, he pushed the hair from the woman's face. She was barely a teenager—like his oldest.

"How many?"

Pratchett let out a long breath. "I heard twenty-three."

Almost two dozen had died here. Half had been armed to the teeth. Automatic weapons with no penchant for restraint were used to shoot up the place of worship. They had done nothing to stop the massacre in the end. Twenty-three people were dead and there wasn't a trace of the killer in the room.

Something else was missing as well, something Ruiz had a difficult time understanding, let alone comprehending. Blood. He noted the wounds on all the victims, each one surrounded by a black stain on the skin. He saw the cause of death clearly with each body he passed, but there was no blood on the ground and no spatter on the walls.

"All of this," he said, lost in the scene. "All committed by one perp?"

"Evidence supports that theory, sir," a voice called from the right-hand wing of the complex. Detective Arthur Davis wore a heavy overcoat, his hands were deep in his pockets, and he had on a wool hat to cover the lack of hair. His partner, Timothy Mitchell, was the younger of the pair and had a fresh gold shield on his chest. He followed from behind. "How one guy can ginsu everyone, especially this crowd, without taking a bullet is beyond me."

"A blade did all this?" Ruiz asked, though he noted the stab wound on the girl and a number of others upon passing. "Nothing else?"

Both Davis and Mitchell nodded.

"Where's the blood?"

A number of eyes glanced up from their work at the question. All had asked it from their curious looks. Davis crept closer to Ruiz, keeping his voice down.

"That's the thing, Captain. There isn't any. Not here, not in the bedrooms to the right, and not on the bodies in the community center to the left. Not on the floors or the walls or the ceilings. Nothing."

Mitchell shook his head. "We're working on it, sir."

"I know you are. It's just—" Ruiz stopped himself. He knew they were on top of the case. He expected nothing but the best from his team. When it came to a scene like this, though, even the best wasn't enough. He needed something to make sense, to have a clear reason behind these deaths. There were too many strange things in Portents, too many shadows hidden from view, and they terrified him. *I might have to give Harvey a call on this one.*

"Sir?" Mitchell asked.

Ruiz shook his head. "Nothing. You two get back to it. I want to know the second you have a lead on this bastard."

"Will do, sir," Davis said. The two circled the scene. Quiet conversations with the forensics team about their progress covered Ruiz's movements back to the edge of the room where Pratchett stood in wait.

It would take hours to secure the site, and even longer to process every aspect of the building. This was the nightmare. While they worked to understand this incident, the killer had already moved on to the next. Ruiz couldn't let that happen.

But Michelle needed him as well. He didn't have hours. He had promised to return, to handle the work and be back home when the sun rose, for his family and the new baby to come.

"Captain?" Pratchett said, pulling Ruiz back to the room.

"Makes a man question bringing a child into this world, Pratchett," Ruiz said, his tone somber. "What kind of person would do that when there's so much darkness everywhere?"

"The kind that believes in hope, sir. That has faith in a better tomorrow," Pratchett replied.

Ruiz huffed. "A fool, then. A damn fool."

He patted Pratchett on the arm, grateful for his words and his company. He should have been home, should have been there for his family, but he had made another promise long ago—a promise to keep them safe from things like this.

"Walk me through it, room by room," Ruiz said. "I want to see it all."

CHAPTER SIXTEEN

The police cordon was in place when she arrived. She'd noticed the cruisers and the flashing lights halted outside the temple on Salem when she was still three blocks out. Rather than run into them head on, Soriya skirted away from the traffic still pouring into the district at the late hour.

She used the shadows surrounding the park just north of the area to stay out of sight. Once she was clear of pedestrians who were heading over to glimpse the mayhem of the evening, Soriya left the street behind completely. She climbed up the side of a neighboring building and leapt to the temple's rooftop. There, a small landing jutted out overlooking the plate glass windows that provided light to the main hall. The landing was most likely used for cleaning, but for her the small ledge provided the perfect glimpse at the chaos below.

Officers raced in all directions. Forensic analysts collected samples and passed them along only to have another batch ready for the runners. A pair of detectives oversaw the entire operation.

Disgust filled Soriya. To think of a holy place defiled in such a way was abhorrent to her. The sight of the weapons on the floor, of the drug paraphernalia littering the scene, opened her eyes to the truth. Soriya realized the temple had no longer served as a house of worship, but a den of iniquity. The dead were users and pushers, dealers and addicts. They had turned the sacred place into a drug haven.

She had never understood the sensation—the need to rip oneself from the world. They destroyed their bodies all to escape their lives for a brief period of time. When reality kicked back in, they fell even harder, only to hide away from it all again as quickly as possible.

Maybe it was fear. Maybe they weren't strong enough to face the challenges of Portents. Again, Soriya had never considered that lifestyle before. She always went into a situation believing it could be overcome. She sought victory and triumph with each challenge, and she was uncompromising in her resolve—like finding the monster who murdered the poor souls in the temple.

It was on her to find the killer and take them down. That task was what she had worked for ever since she was a little girl. As the Greystone, she was the first line of defense for the city. Mentor trusted her in the role more and more.

But with it came the burden of the job. It wasn't something she'd ever imagined when she had started. The weight of their role in the city fell to her. The task was hers and hers alone. She was only sixteen and this was the only life she had ever known or thought about since the accident stole her past from her— and with it any other future.

What if this is the wrong choice?

She had never given the question voice before, yet the words replayed in her thoughts like a broken record. That was Kali's fault. It never would have even come up prior to meeting the ancient deity. Kali had made her opinion clear that she didn't believe in Soriya's calling: that there was something more she could be doing with her life. Kali believed Soriya deserved something more than a life full of responsibility and obligation.

The doubt ate at her, and the words of the seemingly young woman nagged at Soriya's core. She had never felt that way before. There was only her training, only her desire to help Portents and protect the city from the dangers of myth and legend that found their way into her borders. She sought to be the Greystone. It had been all she'd ever wanted. Now there was doubt and she hated every second of it.

"It's Shiva," a voice announced, shattering the silence on the rooftop landing.

Kali was at her side by the window. Since she'd been so lost in her thoughts, Soriya had failed to hear Kali's approach. She crouched close, careful to keep out of the moonlight shadow cast within the building.

"You..." Soriya started. She stood and backed away from the window. Surprise wore off and frustration took over as she realized what Kali meant with her announcement. "You knew. This whole time. Is that why you showed up at the animal shelter tonight?"

Kali sighed, then joined Soriya. "I don't know. I mean, yes, that was what I was thinking at the time. I guess I hoped you'd stumble on him and take care of it for me, but—"

"You're unbelievable!" Soriya exclaimed. Everything became clear to Soriya. From the moment Kali had saved Soriya from the Tengu all the way to the present. Kali had manipulated her from the beginning. Every word said had been to gauge her for the task, to set her up against the monster loose in the city. Soriya turned to leave.

Kali called her back. "Hey! That might have been why we met, but it wasn't why I asked you to the club." She circled around the wounded teen. The ribbon along her wrist whipped in the wind. "Come on, Soriya. I thought you could use some fun."

"While people were dying," Soriya snapped as she pointed to the window.

"Drug dealers," Kali said with a huff. "Not *real* people."

"Don't justify it." Soriya groaned with frustration and crossed her arms over her chest. "I can't believe you."

Kali had pushed a friendship she had no intention of reciprocating. Soriya had hoped to find a kinship with her, someone to share the struggle with. What surprised her was that she had never realized her role *was* a struggle until she met the like-minded woman. The truth was Kali had needed her. She had set Soriya up for this confrontation. *Shiva.* That was the threat in her city. That was the murderer among them. Kali had been aware of him the whole time.

Soriya took a long breath. Her arms fell to her sides. "Tell me about Shiva."

"I'm sure you already know the stories."

"The Destroyer," Soriya said. "Part of the Hindu trinity with

Brahma and Vishnu. Though they stand as creator and protector, Shiva is meant to destroy the universe in order to re-create it."

Kali offered a sarcastic clap. "And now he's here in Portents. You can guess what that means."

"Great," Soriya muttered. A Tengu had proven to be a challenge to her. How was she supposed to tackle a god bent on destroying the world?

Before she could ask the question, a voice called from the far side of the landing, "Now tell us the rest of it, Kali."

Both turned to see Mentor at the edge of the rooftop. His tan cloak billowed in the breeze. His steps were slow to meet them in the center as his right leg continued to fight against him. It had been that way ever since the Minotaur. The injury brought him pain, though he never shared his troubles with Soriya. He never let on the level of agony he endured, though she always knew.

He was supposed to take it easy in the Bypass chamber. Mentor had sent her to the city to tackle the Tengu, a statement of his complete faith in her ability. If he was in the city it was because he had found out what had happened in the aftermath. He'd learned about Soriya's sudden and illegal driving lesson. Panicked at his arrival, Soriya tried to cut him off.

"Mentor, I can explain about—"

"We can talk about your unlawful jaunt after this is over," Mentor said. He smirked at her. Both of them had let anger and frustration guide them in the past. It nearly broke them apart. She was grateful at the new approach. "I do believe you're not the only guilty party."

Kali's hand fell to her hip. "Good to see you again too, Stony."

"Stony?" Soriya asked.

The smirk faded to a grimace. "An unfortunate nickname. One I was hoping had been forgotten. Why are you still in Portents, Kali?"

"I must like the ambiance," she replied. "It sure ain't the people."

"Still treating life as a joke," Mentor said with a nod.

Soriya stayed silent on the sidelines. She couldn't believe Mentor had a prior relationship with the woman she had just met. More than that, she couldn't believe he had never mentioned Kali before. She and Mentor had spent almost every waking moment of the last decade together. He had shared so much of his adventures, of the trials he'd survived as the Greystone. Yet, Kali had never been mentioned. What else could Mentor have been hiding? What else did he keep secret from her and why?

"And you've still got that stick rammed right up your—"

Soriya jumped in before the fight continued. "Care to clue me in on your relationship?" Kali turned away at the question. Soriya faced her teacher with wide eyes. "Stony?"

Mentor rubbed at the thin beard on his cheeks.

Kali was the first to respond. "I helped out your teach here a few times over the years. What was the last one? The Karkadann? No, it was that Yeti thing."

"Dangers attracted by *your* presence in the city."

Soriya stopped. "Wait. Is that why Shiva is here? He's here for you?"

"It doesn't matter," Kali said. "You can't stop him. No one can." Kali shuffled toward the ledge, overlooking the street below.

Soriya moved to press, then hesitated. She decided to join Mentor at the skylight instead. Her teacher fell silent, his gaze shifting from detail to detail. She loved to watch him work.

"He's preparing for something," he said. He caught her staring and pointed to the woodwork surrounding the dead inside the temple. "There's no blood."

"How is that possible?"

Mentor stood and headed for the edge of the rooftop. He grabbed Kali's shoulder and spun her around. "What is he planning?"

"Back off!" Kali pushed him away.

"This isn't a game," Mentor snapped. "Multiple homicides, yet not a drop of blood. What has Shiva brought with him?"

"The demon blade!" Kali bellowed. "He has the demon blade. That's why there's no blood. It absorbed every last drop."

"For what?"

"What the hell does it matter?" Kali said. "Didn't you hear me before? You can't stop him."

"Kali…" There was fear in the woman's eyes. Soriya tried to reach her, tried to connect as they had earlier, but found only coldness.

"Right," Kali whispered. "You have to try. Well, you're going to need help."

"Urg?" Soriya asked.

Kali scoffed. "Tall, green, and gruesome? No, kid. When dealing with an instrument of death you look for another."

"I don't—" Soriya started.

Mentor cut her off. "That is never a good idea, Kali. And where would you—?"

She clenched her fists and dropped them to her sides. "Dammit, Stony. It's the only shot I can think of."

Mentor fell silent, doubt in his gray eyes.

Soriya inched close to Kali. Her hand fell on Kali's shoulder. "Where?"

Kali stared out at the city, beyond the flashing lights surrounding the temple. "The coroner's office."

CHAPTER SEVENTEEN

This wasn't what he had been hoping to find when he returned to the city. Ruiz had counted on some surprise paperwork, a dozen reports he had forgotten about in his absence, or maybe a personnel issue or two. Twenty-three dead in a closed Hindu temple never made the list, nor had the killer still on the loose.

Ruiz stopped short of the front entryway. He leaned against the wall, hand pressed tight to the paneling for support. His eyes closed for a long moment as he tried to rub the exhaustion away. Michelle had been right. He should have stayed at home and made her the priority. Now Portents needed him and he wasn't sure *how* he would break away, not with a monster in his city.

"Captain?"

Ruiz let go of the wall and straightened his back. His eyes snapped open and he cleared his throat to face the voice calling from behind him.

"Yes?" He recognized the officer, a newer recruit to the precinct named Danvers. He was a little too glib with the job, but always showed up when it counted.

"You all right, sir?" Danvers asked. Another officer approached at the sound of their conversation. Both held the same concern in their faces. "Can I call a car for you?"

"I'm fine," Ruiz answered. He wasn't. No one could be fine in a place filled with the dead, but he hated showing it to his officers. He was meant to be *their* strength, not the other way around. Still, he was grateful to have them at that moment.

"Keep up the good work."

"Yes, sir."

They hesitated for a second, then returned to the main atrium of the temple. What was once a place of worship had become a mass grave. Ruiz had to get out of there. He needed the fresh air of the late winter night to cleanse him of the smell of decay.

Mitchell and Davis had things covered. It was *their* case, and while they weren't Greg Loren, they were more than capable of processing the scene. The more important task had become damage control. Members of the press lined the police cordon at the end of the block. The department required a story to tide over the masses while they hunted a madman in their city.

Reporters shouted for his attention as he exited the temple, but he ignored their cries for a headline. He had none to give, none that warranted attention. His focus was on hiding the terror he felt in his gut. They needed to move quickly now. The situation had escalated from the incident at the docks, and if his intuition was right, this was outside their wheelhouse to begin with. They needed to find this monster, post his image on every outlet, and flush him out into the open.

Right now the police had nothing to offer the city but fear. That wasn't an option in Ruiz's mind. The citizens needed reassurance, not terror. When he reached the cordon, he turned his back to the line of press and grabbed Pratchett by the shoulder. The lanky officer spun on his heels in surprise. After being relieved of his post, Pratchett followed Ruiz to the far side of the block.

"Sir?"

"Mitchell and Davis are almost through," Ruiz said. He led the trusted officer toward the line of cruisers parked around the corner, including his personal ride. "Forensics will need some time, but after that I want the place locked down."

"Yes, sir."

Ruiz stopped as he caught Pratchett's flitting gaze. "I'm serious, John. The press is going to be hungry for what happened here. We can't let them in on this, at least not yet. I'll have Central write up a release for them. Until then? We can't have any leaks. Make sure everyone is on the same page."

Pratchett nodded. A verbal response wasn't necessary. Both knew the stakes, and both had seen the devastation inside the temple. Thankfully, the cordon kept everyone to the front of the building. There was an exit along the side that allowed the coroner's staff to remove the bodies without being spotted. Four wagons blocked all view as the dead were laid inside for transport.

Ruiz tried not to watch as the body bags were piled into the wagons. Twenty-three people were dead, yet there were no answers. Anger took over from sadness.

"I want to know the names of every victim. I want to know their friends and family. Hell, I want to know their favorite damn color."

"What could do this?" Pratchett asked. "Who could—?"

"Add it to the list, Pratchett," Ruiz said. He reached his car and opened the door. It creaked loudly under his hand. "Put Danvers and Sloane on it. I want everyone working together on this."

"Where are you heading?"

Home should have been his answer. His wife needed him. His family was counting on him to follow through on a promise—just one promise. Yet... the dead demanded his attention. Michelle would have to wait.

"I'll follow the bodies back to Central for processing. See if we can't solve this before more drop."

"We'll catch him, sir."

"Your words to God's ears, Pratchett," Ruiz said. "Get to it."

The officer gave a slight nod, then started back to the crime scene. Pratchett was a good man—naïve and aloof as hell, but he was committed to helping Portents. Ruiz needed that commitment tonight. He needed every man and woman at the precinct helping on this. He needed it solved so he could head home to his wife and his waiting promise.

He leaned against the car and pulled out his phone. No messages. No texts. A sigh of relief escaped him. "At least one front is calm tonight."

If only he had stayed at home. Everything would have been better had he never left. Sleep sounded heavenly. But there were almost thirty souls that demanded justice.

"What the hell is happening to this city?" he said to the night sky. This wasn't about a killer, not one his people were equipped to handle. This was something else, much as he hated to admit it. It had to be.

To answer his rumination, three shadows slipped from the roof. They dropped to the street and landed at the far end of the block with silent precision. The trio headed away from the flashing lights and the throng of people gathered at the temple. Ruiz immediately recognized the figure in the middle of the group right before they disappeared into the night.

He hadn't seen the man in many years. Ruiz had preferred it that way. "Why the hell didn't I stay in bed?"

CHAPTER EIGHTEEN

The morgue was empty. The transports were still six blocks out, and the night shift had all been called to the scene to handle so many dead. Mentor led Kali and Soriya inside, yet he failed to understand why they were there in the first place.

The basement of the precinct was dimly lit, more like a dungeon than a place of investigation. Rumor had it the city was looking at alternate locations for the morgue to keep it away from the busy traffic of downtown. The truth was, everyone in the building wanted the dead as far away from them as possible. The cops stationed above had always hated the notion of the dead under their feet. As he walked between the slabs prepped for examination, Mentor agreed wholeheartedly.

The moment they arrived, Kali took off. Mentor could only watch as Kali searched frantically through the space, ducking into closed offices that lined the right-hand wall. From there, she moved through the lab and testing areas to the rear of the room. Desperation filled every glance and there was terror in every step. Mentor had never known the woman to be anything but aloof—always needing that next drink or shot of adrenaline to maintain a joyful existence. It worried him.

Soriya's concern, however, took precedence. She held back with him upon their entrance to the morgue. She kept turning toward him with the words on her lips, unable to find the right way to say them.

"You're quieter than usual, little one," Mentor said to break the silence. He continued to monitor Kali's movements.

"Not sure what to say," Soriya answered. There was disappointment in her voice. "Care to tell me any more about your friend here?"

"I could ask the same thing," he said. "I don't recall carjacking as part of our training together."

"About that," Soriya said. She rubbed her neck. "I—"

"Kali can be a great many things, Soriya. A fierce warrior. A powerful ally. What she *chooses* to be is something else entirely." He took a long breath. He had more to say, angry words over his student's choices on the night. But anger had only ever split them apart. He needed her at her best. That only happened when she was with him instead of against him. "She is quite adept at reading people, but also at influencing them. She pushes them to act the way she would in a given situation. I don't blame you for falling for her manipulations, little one."

"She didn't manipulate me, Mentor," Soriya said in irritation. "I wouldn't just... I didn't... Damn."

Soriya bowed her head in surrender, and Mentor patted her shoulder. "Let's move past it, shall we?"

"Please."

He smiled and led her deeper into the morgue. Kali continued her search. Doors slammed with each office visited. Department officials had their names etched into the glass of each one. The Head Coroner's, Hady Ronne's, was most prominently in view. Mentor read each in turn, but still could not fathom why they had come.

Instead, he focused on the bodies which rested before him. Six bodies were covered from viewing on examination tables. He lifted the cloth from the closest one for a better look at a middle-aged man with a scar on his chin. A single puncture wound to the chest appeared to be the cause of death.

"They're the same," Mentor muttered. "They have the same wound as those at the temple, but these victims aren't from that scene."

"Mentor?"

He ignored his student's concern. He dropped the sheet, then moved for Kali to cut her off from her search. "Were you aware there were more deaths?"

"Stony—"

"Enough, Kali!" Mentor shouted. "Were you?"

She refused to meet his glare. Kali continued to peer around the room for signs of life. It was admission enough for Mentor. "Why is it so empty here? Where is she?"

"Kali? Who are you looking for?" Soriya called from the middle of the room. Her hands played with the edges of her leather coat. She was getting antsy—the lack of knowledge had that effect on her.

Mentor felt the same. He grabbed Kali's shoulder and spun her toward him, then locked his hands on her to keep her in place. "Who were you expecting?"

"I can tell you who *I* was expecting," a voice boomed from the elevator lost in the shadows on the far side of the space. A man stepped into the light, his sidearm raised at the strangers in the morgue. Fury filled his eyes, but that was always how Mentor saw Captain Ruiz. "Sure as hell wasn't any of you. Put your hands where I can see them!"

Soriya immediately pivoted from her position. Her fists clenched and she prepared to leap at the newcomer to the room.

"Soriya, don't!" Mentor yelled. He rushed to her side to calm her down, but his knee locked up in mid-step. He reached for support on a nearby slab. The knee was getting worse. Nothing he did seemed to bring it back to full strength—not the daily stretching regimen nor the exercise to build up the muscle around the joint. The Minotaur's blow had done lasting harm, and Mentor had yet to come to grips with what it meant for the future he had seen in the Bypass.

Soriya offered him a helpful hand and he gave her a grateful nod. Then he turned toward the officer. "Ruiz."

The captain squeezed the grip of his department-issued weapon. "You. I thought that was you at the scene. Who are they?"

"Friends. We're trying to—"

"Can the chit chat," Kali interrupted. "Where is she?"

"Who?" Ruiz asked.

"Ronne," Kali pressed. "Hady Ronne. We need to see her."

The Head Coroner? Curious eyes followed Kali's frantic movements to the closed office door. Everyone in the room demanded an explanation as to how a city employee could help stop the murderer currently plaguing Portents.

"She was called upstate to help on a case," Ruiz said. "She's been there all week."

Kali's shoulders slumped. "No."

"Why?" Mentor asked. He was tired of the game, and tired of following instead of leading. None of this was getting them any closer to Shiva. "What were you after here, Kali?"

"It doesn't matter," she replied. She ran her hands over her face and back through her hair. "There's no help here."

Soriya moved for her new friend, but Mentor waved her down. They had asked enough. Kali had never been forthcoming when it came to information. They couldn't afford that. Not with bodies dropping like rain. Mentor turned to Ruiz.

"These victims. Where did they come from?"

The captain bit his lower lip in hesitation. They had never had the best of relationships. Their introduction had been forced through circumstance. Ruiz's inability to accept the true nature of Portents remained because of that initial encounter. When Ruiz had found out the truth he had felt betrayed by his home. Instead of opening his eyes to the wonder surrounding them, Ruiz had closed them off completely.

"Captain," Mentor said, hoping to push past their differences. "I... *We* are trying to help."

"Help. Right," Ruiz said. He jammed his sidearm into the holster on his hip. "These bodies are from the docks. The call came at about 10:30. Cause of death is the same as the temple murders. The killer used some kind of blade, but for some reason no blood was present at the scene."

Kali kept her eyes to the ground. She had already shared the instrument used in the deaths of the men and women found at the temple. The demon blade. Mentor had never heard of it in the lore. He hated the unknown.

"There was more," Ruiz said.

"More?" Mentor asked.

"We found... a door," the captain continued. "This green light surrounded it. It wasn't connected to any building or structure. Just in the middle of the docks. I don't... I don't even know what the hell it was."

A door. Soriya's eyes widened at the mention. They both realized the implications. The color alone was a tip-off, but they had had dealings with doors recently.

One had been used to release the Minotaur into the city. Not a physical door, as Ruiz described, but a gateway that had pierced the wall of the labyrinth and connected the maze to Portents. Could there have been another one? Could the same person have opened another door and allowed Shiva entrance to their world?

"Can you take us there?"

"Not until you tell me what the hell it is that's running loose in my town," Ruiz spat.

Mentor held his tongue. He had seen what true knowledge had done to people, Ruiz included. Soriya, however, was clueless and stepped forward. "Shiva."

"Who?"

"A god of destruction," she said. "He—"

Mentor stopped her from continuing with a thin look. "He is a danger to everyone in Portents, Captain."

"Do you know how to stop him?"

Silence filled the room. The message was clear. Ruiz let out a long breath, then finally nodded toward the elevator. Mentor moved to follow. He stopped when he realized Soriya remained behind in the center of the room.

"Soriya?"

"I'll stay with Kali."

Ruiz waited at the elevator, watching them closely. Soriya shifted to Mentor's side. His hand fell on her shoulder.

"Are you sure, little one?"

"She knows more about what's going on," his student said with a nod. "I'll be okay."

"I know you will. Still—"

"You be careful too," Soriya said. "A door could mean—"

"Exactly. That's why I have to close it."

The car dinged and the elevator doors opened. Ruiz stepped inside. "You coming or not?"

Mentor squeezed Soriya's shoulder then headed to the waiting elevator. "Coming."

They both had their paths to follow. They both knew their task. Shiva had to be stopped.

CHAPTER NINETEEN

Frustration won out. When the elevator closed and the pair of authority figures departed the room, all patience left Kali. Every ounce of frustration at the arrival of Shiva flew out of her in a rage on the room. Tools and equipment crashed to the floor. An unholy scream erupted and filled the room. It masked her trembling hands as she cleared the computer from a workstation. A keyboard and other external devices smashed at her feet.

"Dammit!" she bellowed. "A waste of time!"

She pounded her fists on the table, and then kicked at the drawers. Unfulfilled, Kali lifted the desk and sent it flying into the corner. Beakers and specimens shattered. It wasn't enough. She moved for the next station and found Soriya blocking her path. Kali raised her fist to strike the teenage obstacle, then stopped herself. Her chest heaved in anger as she fought to slow her pulse. Gradually, she relaxed. Her fist lowered and Kali leaned against the tiled wall, sliding her way to the cold ground.

"Why?" she asked as she tucked her head between her knees. "Why the hell did he have to be here? Why did it have to be now?"

Hady Ronne had been her one and only shot. When dealing with a destructive force of nature like Shiva, the only play was to put someone else in their path. Kali's first instinct had been Soriya. Having met her, having talked with her and been in her presence, Kali realized that was the wrong move. She liked Soriya. Part of her had from the moment they'd said hello in their own unique way. She couldn't send the kid to her death like that. Not against Shiva. Not if there was another way.

Ronne held a secret no one else knew about—even Mentor, which Kali found pretty surprising, given the man's nature to know everything about everyone. Ronne's power could have turned the tide against Shiva. Instead, she was absent from the fight completely.

Kali beat her head lightly against the wall at her back. There were no other options. Shiva was powerful enough, but with the demon blade in his hand, the chances of stopping him went from highly unlikely to hopelessly impossible. She needed to run, needed to get far away from Portents.

Soriya, however, continued to block her path. "Did you get the tantrum out of your system?"

The teen held out her hand and Kali accepted the assistance. She stood but remained close to the wall with her back pressed against the cold. She let the chill flow through her to center her. It wasn't enough. Nothing they did was going to be enough against Shiva.

"He has the demon blade, Soriya," Kali said. "Do you understand what that means?"

"No," Soriya replied, her tone sharp and impatient. "Not for a lack of trying either."

"Cute."

"I'm trying to help," Soriya said. "I need you to talk to me."

Kali pushed away from the wall and her companion, and then began to pace the room with brisk steps. Each movement took her to the dead. She circled each in turn. Kali lifted the cloth covering them, letting Soriya see Shiva's victims.

The puncture wounds were clear of blood, the skin as well. All that remained on the surrounding flesh was a small black stain around the entry point. Kali pointed to one.

"Shiva's targeting sinners," Kali explained. "He's using the demon blade to absorb their sin."

"That's what the marking is on the skin?"

Kali nodded.

"Why?"

"To summon the Raktabija—the great demon from the void. Shiva's planning to wash the world clean and transform the future."

"What?" Soriya said. "How?"

"The merest touch," Kali said. "The Raktabija is power incarnate. In an instant, the demon steals the darkness of your soul, from the smallest of sin to the greatest. Nothing is left to chance. It burns through you and leaves nothing but ash in its wake."

"How close is he?"

"I don't know."

Soriya shook her head and crept closer. "Does he have what he needs already? Can he bring this thing to Portents?"

"*I. Don't. Know!*" Kali yelled.

Outside, the transports had arrived. Through the winding halls of the basement morgue they could hear the sound of opening doors and footsteps. Staffers were starting to unload the dead from the temple for examination. It was time for Kali and Soriya to depart.

Soriya blocked Kali's path. The goddess grimaced, her fists clenched at her sides. She shifted across the aisle for another path to the elevator, but the teen followed suit, impeding all movement.

Kali hated her for it. She hated the strength she saw in her new companion's eyes. After everything she had heard, Soriya should have been running for the exit and the earliest flight out of Portents. Instead, a fire burned in her deep brown irises. She wanted the fight. More than that, she clearly wanted to win the fight. Her resolve made Kali hate Soriya all the more.

She couldn't face Shiva. In the thousands of years they'd shared, Kali had never been able to face the destroyer. It would have meant the end of everything she had lived for, every moment of delight and frivolity. Kali refused to face that possibility.

"Move aside, Soriya. I'm leaving."

"That's fine. After you answer my questions," Soriya said.

"You don't get it."

"Yes, I do," Soriya snapped. "I do, Kali. But what if he doesn't have enough?"

"What?"

"What if Shiva doesn't have what he needs to bring the Raktabija to Portents?" Soriya asked and caught Kali's eyes. "Where would he go? If Shiva needs sinners, where would his next target be?"

CHAPTER TWENTY

The gate to Caldwell Correctional clinked shut behind Dennis Holcomb's Suburban as he entered the compound. It existed separate from the rest of the city. Behind the structure was Rose Riley Forest, which stretched to the north, and to the south was the single highway that entered the city limits.

The prison stood as a microcosm away from it all. As warden, Dennis sought to keep it that way. There were no escapes, nor were there scandals that demanded the attention of outside agencies. He ran a tight ship and had personally selected every member of his team. He had people to conduct background checks, staffers who assisted with the paperwork required by the state or federal government, but he always took pride in double and sometimes triple-checking everything.

The sun still sat low in the sky. The shadows of the forest loomed over the prison. Lights shone from the watchtowers on the corners of the structure, and spotlights beamed in standard search pattern throughout the yard. Two men were stationed per tower—there was never a lapse. Extra guards were always on hand to cover every possible circumstance.

Dennis vacated the Suburban, briefcase in hand. He was careful to hit the locking button on his remote three times for assurance. He no longer had the physicality of his youth, and he was slow to move from the vehicle toward the building because of his widening girth.

Wallace Frederick, a stout black man in uniform, met him at the edge of the lot. "You're here early, sir."

Dennis had made a habit of leaving for work before sunrise

the last few days. The early spring of the previous month had set off a number of construction projects in the city, not the least of which was the RDJ that served as the main artery of Portents. Since he was a member of the Riverfront district, his commute had always been long, but manageable thanks to the eight-lane behemoth that snaked through the downtown area toward the Grove to the west.

"Have to be, Wallace," Dennis replied. He enjoyed the man's company and had grown accustomed to seeing his smiling face upon arrival. Wallace had been one of the longest-lasting guards at Caldwell and had risen through the ranks over the years. "Have you seen how much of the expressway they have torn up? I probably add ten miles to my commute by wrapping around Lowtown."

Wallace nodded. "Afternoon gridlock is even worse. They're saying it might take over a year before everything is back up and running."

Dennis huffed. "Dragging their feet as usual. Anyone using it to their advantage?"

"Of course," Wallace answered. He ushered them inside the gate. Security stood at attention behind protective glass. "Falk has mentioned it as his excuse every day this week. Ramirez, too, even though he comes from the Grove, and completely misses the RDJ. There are plenty more."

Dennis grumbled and rubbed at his brow. He placed his bag on the conveyor belt for scanning, then he slipped through the metal detector before collecting his belongings. Wallace joined him after waving at the crew behind the glass.

"Give them a warning," Dennis said. "By next week, I don't want to hear about it again. Got it?"

"Yes, sir."

Dennis grinned and hit Wallace's arm playfully. "So you tell that wife of yours to let you out of bed a few minutes sooner or you're out of a job."

Wallace laughed. "You know her, sir. All hands."

"I saw enough at the Christmas party," Dennis admitted. "Lucky man."

"I tell her every chance I get," Wallace said.

"Smart too," Dennis said.

They cut left to the support building attached to the prison. Cold concrete and bars faded behind them. Carpet took over with offices on each side for meetings and outside visitors. Wallace led the way to the end of the corridor and opened the door. The space widened to a large lobby. Three desks were positioned inside—two on the right and one on the left. They made up Dennis' inner circle: a secretary for calls and appointments, an assistant to draw up paperwork, and a personal guard to accompany him on his rounds through the structure. Everything was in its place and Doris, his secretary, was inside waiting for their arrival.

"Morning, Warden Holcomb," Doris said. She shuffled paperwork to the side, straightening up her organized chaos. Her mornings always started that way, but somehow she managed to clear every task by the end of her shift. Her attention to detail constantly impressed him. "Can I get you—?"

"Coffee, Doris," Dennis said. He turned to his escort. "Talk to you later, Wallace."

The guard nodded and returned to the corridor. "Sir."

By the time Dennis reached the door to his office, Doris was by his side with a steaming cup of liquid energy. "Here you are."

"Thank you, dear," he said, taking the beverage. "Incident report?"

Doris held up a finger, then returned to her desk. A green report stuck out from the pile and she pulled it loose. After glancing over the document, she passed it over.

"A light one," she commented. "Must be your birthday."

Dennis chuckled. "More like a lunar eclipse."

Despite everyone being locked away in their cell, and the tight ship being run at Caldwell, the days never stayed light. There were disciplinary actions to settle between inmates. Lawyer demands on both sides of the aisle constantly needed scheduling or haranguing between multiple parties. There was always something to be handled or addressed, and everything ran through his hands at one time or another.

Dennis took the light incident report in hand, while wondering how long it would last. He clutched his coffee in his right hand, while his other hand opened the office door. He paused in the frame. "I'm expecting Spaulding from the state to arrive at ten. I'll be playing catch up until then."

"Very good, sir."

Dennis shrugged. "We'll see what demands the state has before we make that determination."

He closed the door to his mini-sanctuary and took a breath. Exertion from the walk and the multiple streams of queries that seemed to rise from everyone around him always left him drained. The coffee would help. So would the silence of the office. He circled his desk and let his bag settle along the side. He savored a short sip of the steaming beverage.

"Peace and quiet," he said to the darkness of the room. He clicked the small desk lamp to illuminate the office.

A shadow grew in the corner of the room. "A rare treat, I take it."

Dennis' chair almost tilted over as he shook from the sound of the stranger's voice. "Who the hell?"

The figure stepped into the light. Dennis blinked at the sight of the man. He wore no shirt, and his skin was tinted in a pale shade of blue. The figure crept closer, his right hand wrapped tight along the hilt of what appeared to be a sword.

"Not another move," Dennis said. He leaned against the edge of his desk. His fingers slowly shifted toward the silent alarm trigger beneath his seat. "I can have a dozen guards in here in seconds."

The man raised his weapon and let it settle across his palms. "And they would meet an unjust end. Swiftly."

"I said—"

The figure shook his head, which caused Dennis to fall silent. The stranger took a seat across from him. "You will do no such thing, for you do not wish to see so many fall this day. What you *will* do is sit and listen to my offer."

"Your offer?" Dennis asked. He couldn't stop staring at the man's weapon. The stranger motioned for the chair behind the desk. Dennis' finger hovered before the panic button, then fell away. He took the chair and sat against the soft leather. "If I refuse?"

"You won't," the figure assured Dennis. The stranger sheathed the sword as he leaned forward. His pale eyes swallowed the warden, stealing his hope. "You will help me. Truly, it is the only choice you have."

CHAPTER TWENTY-ONE

"Incredible."

The door was real. It stood before Mentor and Ruiz, hidden from view between the outcropping of buildings and cargo containers that ran the length of the docks. The opening rested above the wooden planks and stood six feet tall. Storage sheds for equipment to maintain the boats in the summer were positioned on both sides. Before them, the door glowed in a green hue Mentor immediately recognized.

The Bypass. The portal was somehow connected to the mystical orb tucked beneath the surface of the city. Shimmering within the mists were other realms. The door connected to different worlds and times. It had brought Shiva to this place. *Someone* brought him to Portents.

"Not the word I would have used," Ruiz said. He kept his distance, letting Mentor take the lead in the thin alcove. Ruiz had never cared for the life. When he had met Mentor, the truth about Portents had been forced upon him. Ruiz had fought it with every fiber of his being. Some things hadn't changed, no matter the years passed. "You've seen this kind of thing before?"

Mentor hesitated, unsure what to share. How much did Ruiz want to know? How much could he possibly accept? Mentor ran the details through his own thoughts again.

He *had* seen something similar before, but never to this extreme. Previously, when the Minotaur had pierced the veil and escaped the labyrinth, the opening had been locked to one location. It had been merely a gateway, not a fully functioning door.

This, however, was a direct connection to the Bypass; it was an impossibility from everything he understood.

The truth was, he had never understood enough about the Bypass, the Greystone, or anything in the world he professed to protect. The Bypass, its origin and true purpose, remained a mystery. Yet someone had managed to reach into it and pull a portion of the energy contained within the Bypass to build a doorway. Pillars within the underground chamber locked the Bypass in place, yet somehow this portal had become a free-standing link.

On one hand, yes, he had seen it done before. But to this degree? No one had ever seen that.

"How many others know about the door?"

"A few," Ruiz said. Mentor turned away in surprise. "They brought the information straight to me. I asked them to keep it cordoned off from the others and to keep it quiet."

Six had died at the scene. Added to the dozens at the temple, the events of the night took the word massacre to another level. Shiva destroyed all in his path, and he was currently carving his way across the city unimpeded. Nothing seemed capable of halting his progress.

"I appreciate that," Mentor said. He faced the door once more. His hand reached to the pouch on his hip and removed the small object locked inside. The Greystone was warm to the touch, almost burning compared to the chill left by the late-winter air. He felt the energy coursing up his arms as he pointed the elemental tool at the portal.

He had never attempted anything like it before. The door was a piece of the Bypass. It was never meant to roam free from the rest. Someone, either incredibly talented or a walking catastrophe waiting to happen, had proven him wrong. Now he needed a way to put the genie back in the bottle.

"What are you—?"

Mentor shook his head, silencing Ruiz. Focus was required to wield the power of the stone. The door shifted and faded. The green glow dimmed, then snapped in little flicks of light. They rose like fireworks before dissipating against the night sky.

The door collapsed and darkness returned. Mentor's arms fell, the weight of the stone immense from the effort. His chest heaved for breath. The effort had almost been too great. Sweat dripped from his hair as if he had been in a sauna, like the attempt had lasted hours instead of seconds.

"Hey, are you okay?"

Mentor nodded, then he shuffled to the side of the nearest storage shed and slid to the ground. "It used to be easier."

"That?" Ruiz asked. He circled the scene for signs of the door's former position. There was nothing. No remaining energies. It was gone. If only Shiva could be handled in the same fashion. Ruiz rubbed his eyes, then moved for the opposite storage shed for support. "Nothing about this seems easy."

"I suppose not."

"Is that what she does now, too?" Ruiz continued. Irritation rose in his voice. "That girl at the morgue? Soriya?"

"Yes," Mentor replied. "I've been teaching her."

"A child," Ruiz said. "You've been teaching her what, exactly? How to die at the hands of one of these damn monsters? Are you insane?"

Mentor struggled to stand, but his knee threatened to buckle from the effort. "Soriya is more than capable."

"Don't give me that crap," Ruiz snapped. "No kid should be involved in this world. The things you've seen? Hell, the deaths tonight alone. What kind of father would—?"

"*Teacher*," Mentor said, unwilling to back down. "I'm her teacher. And she's proven herself time and time again capable of handling the challenges to come…"

After I die. He almost said it—like it was a matter of fact statement, an absolute. He knew it was. On some level, he'd known the truth the moment he saw the vision in the Bypass. He was going to die. Not as a withered old man, not after decades of watching over Soriya. It was coming much sooner than that. He was going to leave her alone with the burden of the Greystone. She would have no one else, no connection like the one he had offered her so many years ago.

Had he done enough? Had he prepared her for that future? Could he ever *truly* do enough to make her ready for when he was gone?

"You put it on her," Ruiz said. He was clearly lost to his anger, not recognizing Mentor's absence from the debate. Ruiz was a family man. He fought for his children and saw nothing more than that in the faces of everyone else in Portents: someone to protect and shield from the world. "Did she ever *really* have a choice in the matter? Did she even know what she was getting into when you pulled her into your world?"

"Someone has to view this city with open eyes."

Ruiz's hands balled up into fists, and he stomped away from Mentor for the end of the pier. "I should lock the lot of you up and forget the whole damn thing."

He had always been circumspect about the world. He always hated how a former colleague, Julian Harvey, had revealed the true city to him. Mentor was there that night. He had seen the fear on the officer's face. He had seen the terror at the secret he would have to keep from everyone. Mentor never realized how much hate Ruiz still carried from their first encounter.

"End this if you can," the tired captain said.

"I will."

Ruiz shook his head, unable to truly believe him. He was unable to even look at him. He turned his back to Mentor. "Just get your disappearing act over with already. I have work to do."

"Very well," Mentor said. "Stay safe, Captain."

Mentor slipped into the shadows of the dock and turned the corner. He didn't go any farther. The port was a dangerous area, and he wanted to make sure Ruiz reached his car.

It took a moment before Ruiz spun around to the silence of the docks. He pulled his coat tighter, frustration slipping from his lips and rising into the cold air in a puff of smoke.

"Stay safe?" Ruiz muttered to the shadows. "Fat chance of that."

The captain headed for his waiting car. Mentor clung to the darkness until Ruiz had reached the driver's-side door. Then Mentor started in the opposite direction for the city. The gateway had been secured, the Bypass closed off from whoever had managed to manipulate the energies within.

For now.

Two incursions had occurred using the same method. Someone was playing a dangerous game. Worse, they were learning from each experience. Mentor feared the next attempt. But that would only come if Shiva was dealt with. Soriya was working with Kali to figure out a path to victory, and he had to do the same in his own way. He needed to find out where the destroyer was in his city.

For that, there was only one place to turn.

The Bypass.

It was time to ask another question. No matter what the answer might be.

CHAPTER TWENTY-TWO

What was he thinking? How could that lunatic think to bring a child into *this* world? The questions followed Ruiz all the way to his car. Through the gloom of the night, he still felt the so-called Greystone's presence. He never learned another name for the mysterious stranger that had dogged his career for over a decade now.

There were horrors in Portents, monsters constantly lurking in the shadows. To think differently was ignorance at best, and most likely delusional. To allow a child to face that, even a teenager, was flat-out wrong on every level. The threat of death would be nonstop and the only possible ending for her.

"Dammit," Ruiz grumbled. He opened the door to his car and slipped inside. The frame groaned under him, the car long since past its prime. He closed the door behind him and settled into the seat.

He needed to go home. There was nothing for him to do now. The Greystone and his protégé were on the case. For a second, Ruiz truly believed it was the better solution. He would let them face the danger and allow the burden to fall on someone capable of understanding. His people, the dedicated officers of the Central Precinct, had no clue what this was about. They were hunting a murderer, not this Shiva person.

A god of destruction. When did phrases like that become possible to Ruiz?

He sank deeper into the cushion. Locking the door, Ruiz shut his eyes for a well-deserved break. Just a five-minute respite from the storm.

It failed to take hold. Sleep stood against him just like everything else. The Greystone had asked for his trust, for his support, and Ruiz couldn't give it to him. He hated the notion of someone outside the law handling things, even though they might be better prepared for the task. That wasn't who Ruiz was, as a person or an officer.

It was his job.

Ruiz let out a long breath. Before him, the sun began to make the first overtures of the day. Pinks and oranges dotted the horizon over the port. The clouds interspersed in a thin veil over the water. If it had been any other day it might have looked beautiful. All it did now, however, was remind Ruiz of his wife and the sunrises shared as a young couple in love. They used to walk along the docks and dream of a large family. They always imagined an incredible future that would never pull them apart.

Yet that was all he did now. *He* ripped them apart, strengthening the great divide that had infected their relationship for years. Thanks to the Greystone. Thanks to men like Julian Harvey. Thanks to monsters like this Shiva. All of his problems seemed to arrive as if by conveyor belt. One was handled and the next was in place to take over.

Michelle deserved better. It was time to prove that to her. Ruiz reached for his phone, which he had clumsily left in the cup holder on the center console.

There were five missed calls.

"No." He unlocked the device and thumbed his way to the voicemail. Before he could finish, the device rang in his hand. Ruiz's heart stopped for a second. Then he answered and pulled the phone to his ear. "Michelle? What's—?"

"Dad."

"Zoe?" he asked. He tried to shake away his swirling thoughts at the sound of his daughter's voice. "What's—?"

"I've been calling, Dad," Zoe said. "Where are you?"

"I'm…" There wasn't an acceptable answer that would make a damn bit of difference. The fact was, he wasn't at home. Where he should have been for his wife and his children. "What's going on? Is your mom—?"

"The ambulance just took her."

The baby. It was time and he wasn't with her. He'd missed the births of his first two children. Work was always too important. There was always another case to break, another obligation to fulfill, that superseded his own desires. Why hadn't he listened to Michelle last night? Why hadn't he left work to the others? Dozens had been willing to take the burden from him.

"Where is she headed?"

"Mercy," his daughter answered, a tremble in her voice. She was only twelve. Ruiz always seemed to forget, since Zoe acted much older when they were together. "They said they were taking her to Mercy."

"Okay. Good," Ruiz said. He started the car. The engine clicked over twice before roaring to life. It was definitely time for an upgrade. "What about you and your sister?"

"Mrs. Talbot from next door is here," Zoe said. In the background, he could hear Teresa crying and Margie Talbot doing her best to calm her. The sound grew more distant. Zoe must have been moving through the home as she spoke. "Mom called her to take care of us."

"She's a smart lady."

"Are you going to be there, Dad? Mom seemed scared."

Ruiz shifted the car to drive. He put the phone to speaker and set it on his lap. "Heading there now, Zoe. Nothing is going to keep me from being there for them."

Not even a door to another world... He glanced back to the docks and the colors rising along the water. He felt his wife's hand in his and the future ahead of them. He had meant to keep so many promises, yet had let them slip away. He refused to let it happen again.

"Take care of your sister, okay?" Ruiz said into the line. "I'll call soon."

"Love you, Dad."

Ruiz smiled. "Love you too, Zoe."

He hung up and tossed the phone aside. He loved them more than anything in the world. Yet it had never gotten him to walk away from the job. Something had to change; something had to end the lies and the distance that grew with each new murder in Portents.

Ruiz had to make this right for Michelle. For the future of their family. He slammed on the accelerator, rushing north for the hospital.

CHAPTER TWENTY-THREE

Shiva watched the warden depart. Support staff, ranging from the cleaners to the secretary pool, followed closely. The guards were the last to leave, wary of locking the doors on their way out. They had argued with the warden over what was happening, over protocol and procedure, but had eventually acquiesced.

Only one had had to die to make the point clear.

Restraint had been the key in the end. When a man named Wallace had put up a fight for the sake of his colleagues, Shiva made them all watch him die. He did it slowly. He started with a cut along his arm and another on his leg. From there, each slice had been deeper than the last until the final blow across his neck.

When the guards watched their friend die, they'd realized the validity of Shiva's threat. They ran from the corridor, leaving behind complete access to the prison—and the key to Shiva's mission in the world.

He waited until the last car slipped past the gate and the barrier slid back in place before he left the office of the warden. He enjoyed the view, staring down over the yard as if he ruled Caldwell. He imagined it was the warden's outlook as well, powerful and omnipotent.

Turning from the window, Shiva left the offices behind. The departure of the guards had created an absence and the world disliked the void. All it took was one guard to grow a spine and the authorities would come and interfere. If that happened they would fight to the last man. Shiva would slaughter them—of that there was no doubt—but to put that many innocents on his docket tainted his mission. The visceral image sat in his gut like a cancer; the carnage was unnecessary so long as he went about the work.

Carpet faded to cold concrete as he approached the cells. Inmates slammed against bars, and cries of confusion escaped from the multitude. Shiva hesitated at the gate barring him from the general population ward.

The wing was two floors high with cells on both sides and ran in the shape of an L. Those imprisoned in the cellblock were killers and rapists, drug dealers and abusers. They had preyed on the weak, and the law had seen fit to rehabilitate them rather than erase them from society completely. The law had hoped some could eventually hold meaning in their lives and possibly contribute to the well-being of the world.

If only they knew, Shiva thought with a malicious grin on his face. They were about to serve the greatest cause of all: a planet-wide rebirth. It would be a world without sin, without pain. A world transformed for the better. It was his promise to fulfill and the day had finally arrived to make good on it.

An access card the warden had given had provided Shiva un-fettered access to the ward. He closed the gate behind him. Shouts rose from the gallery. The eyes of over two hundred men glared at him. They required answers, but in their fear they turned to jests and insults about his manner of dress and the color of his skin. Humanity was nothing if not predictable in that fashion.

Shiva answered by opening the doors to their cells.

Men staggered into the corridor. The leaders quickly took their place at the head of the conversation.

"What the hell is this, now?" one asked.

"Frank," a squirrelly individual on his right called. "What's he holding?"

They looked hungrily at the access card in Shiva's hand. Shiva let the means for their escape drop to the floor at his feet. Then he stepped over it.

"That, gentlemen, is your ticket to freedom," Shiva pro-claimed loud enough for them all to hear. "All you have to do is get past me."

"Is he insane?" The question was echoed in a dozen murmurs.

"No," the man named Frank answered. "He's confident."

"Don't care," an ape of a man said as he charged ahead. "I can handle this pantywaist."

No one saw the blade strike the man. No one even saw the weapon leave its sheath. They only realized the fight was over by the crash of the man's head on the ground. It rolled to a halt near the cells on the right, the man's eyes still wide open.

"Holy shit!"

Frank stepped forward to quiet the terror. "What is it you want, exactly?"

"You," Shiva said. "All of you. Your hate, your depravity, your lack of a soul. My blade requires every sin and every crude act committed against your fellow man. And I will have it."

Shiva took a step forward. The collective mass of inmates at Caldwell took one back in response. Their strained stares looked for answers or a way out of the madness.

There was only one solution in Shiva's eyes. He led with the demon blade, tinged in the sin of the fallen figure at his feet.

"So, who would like to be my next volunteer?"

CHAPTER TWENTY-FOUR

Caldwell loomed before them. The car ride across town was longer than it should have been. The RDJ was closed. The major artery of the city had been ripped up for a construction project would take years to clean up. The city hadn't handled it well, forcing commuters around the Lowtown district to reach most, if not all, of the main thoroughfares.

Kali drove. The car was another one of her borrows—this time from the precinct lot. Soriya had said nothing about it. Few words had passed between them during the journey, though Kali had made several attempts. She played for a smile, to recapture the energy and frivolity that started their friendship.

A lie had brought them together. Soriya, however, now knew the truth and wasn't easily won over. Kali had manipulated everything about their relationship from the start and nothing could make up for it, though the driver tried her best.

Caldwell was the logical next step for Shiva. If drug havens and random criminal elements couldn't be found, the prison was the only heavily populated area containing everything the god might need to achieve his destiny.

The word stung Kali. She hated the term, hated how it had followed her from the very beginning. When she had arrived in Portents, after she had snuck away from the Svarga Loka that contained her essence, she had hoped to avoid the path laid before her by fate. She had wanted nothing to do with the stories written about her exploits and their end. She always pushed for more time—more fun out of existence. Portents was the perfect haven for her escape. Empty joy had filled her days and nights.

She had loved every second of it.

Or had she?

Soriya was forcing her to question everything. Kali hid her reaction well from the teen, but doubts manifested in her mind. Had she truly enjoyed the emptiness that came with her life? What purpose had she served? What point was there to her time in Portents? There were so many questions, and she disliked every single one of them. She seethed at the effect Soriya had on her after only a few hours together.

Most of all, Kali hated that Soriya might have been right about it all.

The car came to a halt south of the entrance. They parked down the single road that ran the length of the prison. Cars raced from the lot, apparently vacating the grounds as quickly as possible. Guards and support staff alike fled the prison compound without looking back.

"Where the hell are they going?" Kali asked. When she glanced over to the passenger seat for an answer, it was empty. Soriya was already slamming the door shut behind her and moving for the fence surrounding the prison.

Kali unbuckled her belt and joined Soriya. She paused at the front of the car. Lights flashed inside the prison. Kali could feel his presence the moment they arrived. Shiva was in there. They had found him.

"Soriya, wait," Kali called.

The teen's hand rested on the chain-link of the fence. "Thanks for the lift."

She took a step up and Kali pulled her back down. "Come on, Soriya, wait. You don't have to do this. This doesn't have to be your fate. I was wrong to try and pull you in. Let someone else deal with this. Let them—"

"Stop," Soriya snapped. She batted away Kali's hand. There was disgust in her eyes, and more—disappointment. "You know, when we met I had hoped that you would be someone to admire. I thought you would be someone to fight beside, to get strength from to handle this burden."

"I'm *trying* to help you," Kali replied.

Soriya shook her head. "You're only helping yourself. First it was putting me onto this and now, what, you feel guilty? I'm done listening, Kali. I've heard enough."

She turned for the fence once more, then stopped. More flashing lights beamed from behind barred windows. They filled an entire floor before fading as if they'd never existed. Screams could be heard over the rushing wind, brief and terrified, before they disappeared.

"It's him, isn't it?" Soriya asked.

Kali nodded, though her companion failed to see. "Soriya—"

"I have to help."

Kali fell silent. There was nothing more to be said. Soriya had made her choice, and so had Kali. She watched as Soriya took to the fence and climbed. There was no hesitation, no doubt in her movements. People, even though they were nothing more than criminals, needed saving and she was there for them. Careful to avoid the barbed wire along the top, Soriya leapt to the other side and ran at full speed across the yard for the prison wing.

She was inside and out of sight a moment later.

Kali waited near the fence, fingers wrapped tight around the wire separating them. She had been wrong about Soriya, and wrong to force her into this situation. Shiva was too dangerous to face alone. Yet Kali still stood outside it all, unable to make a move. Once, long ago, she had been known as a goddess—worshipped for her lust for life and her destructive presence. Life had stolen that fire, her need for it, and her desire to keep it going for as long as she could. Fear ruled her now.

She started back to the car. Frustration built with each step. Soriya wasn't strong enough, no matter what she believed. She couldn't face Shiva alone.

"Yet she went in there anyway," Kali whispered. Her head slumped to her chest, and her hands settled on the hood of the car. "You coward. You worthless coward. She went in there for you."

Kali looked back to the prison. Lights flashed and men yelled, their terror carried on the wind. Soriya was next, she could feel it. Kali hesitated between the prison and the car, lost in the choice between her life and that of her friend.

CHAPTER TWENTY-FIVE

Soriya couldn't wait any longer. Not after the screams. Shiva was inside the prison; he had beaten them to it. Kali had managed to figure out every step the monster had taken. Still she hesitated to act.

It irked Soriya to no end. She had wanted Kali to be the first to jump into the yard, the first to face the threat. The woman had been so decisive, so confident, against the Tengu. The energy about her inspired Soriya, yet now she saw nothing of that woman in Kali—only her self-involvement and desire for pleasure over substance.

No, there was no more time to wait and hope for a better outcome. Soriya landed in the yard of the prison and raced across for access to the building. She reached the door, but it was locked. Removing the stone at her hip, Soriya cradled it in her left hand. She took a deep breath and closed her eyes.

Strength flowed through her body. Her right hand took hold of the handle and pulled. The lock crumbled from her might, allowing her to slip inside.

Darkness took hold. Emergency lighting was staggered throughout the corridor. She was in the prison proper, with the admin and support buildings to her left. She suddenly understood why everyone had fled. No one wanted to be around when Shiva made his presence known.

The screams were louder now. They rang out from the right, drawing her deeper into the maze of corridors that made up the prison. She passed by offices and break rooms, then skirted through visitation areas and small conference rooms. When she made it to the general population ward Soriya was forced to stop. The gate was locked.

She should have known better. She had rushed inside without a plan, without hesitation, as she always did. Soriya hadn't counted on the amount of preparation and care Shiva had taken with his actions. He had only been in the city for a few hours and had somehow managed a body count in the dozens.

Kali had been right. He was dangerous.

Soriya had to stop him.

She searched the area for a way inside. The screams continued. The wing was shaped like an L and Soriya could see the flashes of light from the opposite side. They lessened, and with them did the cries of the inmates.

Time was against her. A guard station was positioned just outside the ward, but it was locked. Soriya felt her pulse quicken, her heart pumping with adrenaline. The stone was back in her hand and a rune beamed through her fingers.

The door crashed inside the station. Soriya quickly scanned the desks and controls for some guidance. A passkey rested on the ground beneath a chair. She snatched it up and ran it along the scanner on the desk. The master control went from red to green, and the ward was unlocked with a few keystrokes.

Individual cells had been opened and were vacant. There were two floors of inmates in the general population area, with two inmates per cell. There must have been over two hundred men held within the walls of one ward. Two hundred hardened criminals, and Shiva had released them all.

When she rounded the corner, Soriya finally realized why. Though the numbers were clearly against him, Shiva held no fear. He didn't need to worry about being overwhelmed by the prisoners. He had come for a single purpose.

Bodies lay scattered along the floor. Small piles of corpses accumulated in the corners. Most appeared to have attempted to flee from the monster among them. They had never stood a chance.

Hovering above them was a man. His skin was a pale blue and his eyes were bright white. He sat in the air over his victims with his legs crossed. Upon his palms sat a sword with obsidian steel. It pulsed in waves of darkness throughout the blade. Energy surged in his presence, dark and disgusting.

It sickened Soriya. She had never seen such wanton murder. Never had she witnessed such a disregard for human life.

"You… You murdered them all!"

His eyes flashed in recognition and Shiva lowered back to the ground. He grabbed the hilt of the sword and let it settle at his side.

"Of course," Shiva said. His voice was hardened and cold.

"Why?"

"What other choice did I have? Their sins set their path. Fate sets mine."

Soriya shook her head. She held the Greystone before her, hands locked on the weapon. "Fate needs a rewrite, then."

Hellfire surged all around her. It sparked along the tattered clothing of Shiva's victims and the sheets of their beds in the cells surrounding the ward. Every ounce flowed free and shot at Shiva.

Soriya screamed from the effort, focusing her entire will into the stone for more. She had never attempted such a strike, but there was little choice. Shiva had managed to kill everyone around him. He was a force of nature, not a man, and she had to treat him in kind.

Heat surrounded her, and her fingers and hands blistered from the intensity. Her eyes thinned as she squinted through the flames for a sign of her target. Shiva disappeared behind a wall of fire, the world burning around him. When there was nothing left but flames, and after the pressure stole the breath from her lungs, she paused.

The rune dimmed and Soriya staggered, then fell to her knees. The stone was cool to the touch and it soothed her cracked skin while the flames flickered and faded. Shiva should have been lying on the ground—broken and defeated. Instead, he stepped out of the flames, completely unharmed.

"Impossible," she exclaimed.

Shiva merely grinned.

Soriya stood. She squeezed the stone tight to her side and leapt at Shiva with everything she had left.

Even with the additional strength the Greystone offered, it mattered little to Shiva. He swatted away her driving fist with ease and grabbed her by the neck. Fingernails sliced into her throat ever so slightly and a dribble of blood ran along her skin.

"You are not meant for this," Shiva said. He leaned close and took in her scent. "Too pure. Too innocent. You will thank me when this ends."

"Doubtful," Soriya replied. She tried to pry free of his grip, but failed. He squeezed harder, excitement in his eyes.

"Shiva!" a voice cried from the far side of the ward. Both turned to see Kali at the edge of the chaos.

His eyes grew wide to match his grin. "Ah, my dear Kali. I thought I sensed you in this place."

"Let her go," Kali said, though she was slow to approach.

She kept her hands open and in front of her.

Shiva eyed her curiously, then did the same to Soriya. "A connection? Interesting. You continue to surprise me, Kali. Let me return the favor."

He dropped Soriya. She hit the ground on her back. Before she could move, he was over her. The demon blade shot forward and stabbed through her right shoulder, forcing a scream of pain out of Soriya.

"No!" Kali shouted.

Shiva removed the blade. Darkness surrounded the wound and spread in all directions. "She will die, Kali," Shiva announced. "Because of you."

"Damn you, Shiva. None of this was necessary." Kali spread her hands wide, showing Shiva the chaos he had created and the death he had brought to Portents. "You didn't have to do any of it."

"It's my destiny," Shiva replied. He pointed the demon blade at her. "Are you ready to face yours?"

CHAPTER TWENTY-SIX

She had come to help Soriya. The internal debate raged in her thoughts, pulling her in every direction, and begging for an answer when she had none to give. Soriya needed her. The willful teen had no idea of the threat Shiva represented, nor any idea of the danger she had walked into.

Soriya moaned with pain. Her eyes closed and her hand clasped tight to the wound along her right shoulder. Even through her shredded shirt and between her fingers, Kali could see the black tendrils spreading along her skin. Poison took root from the demon blade. Rather than draw out the sin from Soriya, Shiva had inserted a taste of it. It was growing inside her, murdering her by inches.

"Come, my dear," Shiva said, goading her to act on Soriya's behalf. Seeing the teen in so much pain made Kali angry. Her fists clenched and the fight was all she craved—all reason threatened to abandon her. "You know you want to."

It was all Shiva desired as well, and that made the difference for her. Kali hesitated. She refused to let this be the end, to play his game. She couldn't let it end.

"That's what this is, isn't it, Shiva?" She peered around at the dead lining the ward. Small flickers of flame continued to dance from the cells on either side. The bodies were stacked like cordwood. There was no blood. It had all been absorbed by the demon blade, which pulsed with energy. "This was all an invitation, wasn't it? Well, I won't play your game."

Shiva lowered the blade. He looked her over then shook his head. He could see it all, though she tried her best to hide it.

The shaking fear, the tremors in her hands and legs. He saw every ounce of her terror. "So much power in you and still you do nothing? You'll watch the world burn before someone forces you to accept your fate."

The word pushed her over the edge. "Enough of that! You and the others. All you do is play to type. You accept a course that has never done anything for you but lock you in a role. I refuse to accept that. Do you hear me? I refuse, Shiva!"

Shiva nodded. His bare feet left the concrete of the prison ward and he hovered over Kali. His legs criss-crossed like he was sitting on air. The sword was balanced over his lap by his palms. The whites of his eyes beamed brightly in their judgment of her. "Then let the world pay the price for your decision."

He floated along the air toward the exit. His mission had been a success. She could feel the energy rising from the blade. His weapon was filled to the brim, overflowing with the sin necessary for Shiva to reach his goal. He would bring no more chaos to Portents.

Only the end.

Soriya, even through the pain of the wound in her shoulder, reached out to Kali. Her eyes pleaded for the woman to stop the monster before he departed and put more lives at risk. Kali shook her head. She bit her lip, struggling for a way out rather than become trapped in the cycle that was her life. To fight fate.

She turned for the exit. "No. Wait! Shiva, stop!"

He did, slowly spinning to meet her. His head tilted and a curious look spread across his face. "A spark of life?" he said, taunting her. "Is that concern I see for your pathetic protector?"

"She's innocent, Shiva," Kali said. She pointed to Soriya, who struggled for breath. "That's who you're doing this for, aren't you? The innocent of this world? Soriya is one of them."

"She stands against my goals."

"She's trying to help people!" Kali shouted. "She's trying to do what's right!"

"Then she should let me complete my task," Shiva replied. "I have no choice in this, Kali. None of us do. There is only the end of the story to come. We *all* have our parts to play in it."

Soriya was dying. The poison was spreading, winding its way

through her body. She suffered for the sake of others. She wanted Kali to do the same. She wanted Kali to stand up to the menace before them and be fearless.

But all Kali saw was the end of the story. Just like Shiva. However, instead of embracing it, Kali cowered in terror from it.

"The hell with that," she said, her words sharp like knives. She turned away from Shiva and ran for her fallen friend. She cradled Soriya's body close and lifted her from the cold ground. "Your fate. Your damn destiny. The hell with that and the hell with you!"

"Your choice is made, then," Shiva said. "You disappoint me, Kali."

Without another word, Shiva departed. He floated around the corner and out of the ward. Kali was left with nothing but her dying friend and those recently taken from the world. Kali held Soriya close as she started for the exit.

"Come on, kid," Kali said. Soriya's eyes closed, her breathing shallow. Strands of darkness sifted under her skin. It ran in thin lines up her neck and down her arms. The wound pulsed along her shoulder, black puss oozing along the surface. "I need you to talk to me, kid. Show me some of that obstinate superhero dogma you're always spouting."

Kali stopped at the door to the ward. Flashing lights beamed down the corridors, and sirens echoed in the air. The authorities had finally arrived, though they were far too late to do any good.

The same held true for Kali. She had come to help Soriya, to save her from an early demise. Kali had failed in that regard. The demon blade had left Soriya withering and dying.

"Dammit, Soriya. Why couldn't you have listened to me? Why didn't you trust me?"

Footsteps approached. She couldn't be seen here, couldn't risk being taken in for questioning, or for the EMTs to waste their time coming up with a diagnosis for an infection they had no clue how to treat. She had to make this right. She had to save Soriya.

Kali pulled Soriya even closer and fled through the darkness for the yard door that had served as their entrance. It was the only way out, the only hope to make it to safety. Kali was Sori-ya's last hope for survival.

CHAPTER TWENTY-SEVEN

Kali kicked the door in. Urg sat on the couch and jumped at the crashing sound that filled the room. He wore only a pair of shorts, and his hairy chest was exposed. The television was on, tucked in the corner behind the door. The sound of grunting and moaning caused Kali to stop before stepping completely inside.

"What the hell are you doing?" Urg yelled. He scrambled for the remote on the table. Angry eyes remained locked on the intruder, but he turned his body away as he fiddled with the control to mute the television.

"Can it, orc!" Kali answered. She carried Soriya in her arms. The teen's chest heaved, fighting for each breath. Her eyes, though, had long since closed. Darkness ran under her skin like tendrils, all snaking from the wound in her right shoulder. Kali waited for the sound to fade on the television. "I need you to end the special 'me' time you've got going on and help me out here!"

The light from the screen went out. "The couch," Urg said. "Use the—" He grabbed a blanket hanging from the back of the furniture and spread it across the cushions. "Okay, *now* use the couch."

"Gross, man. Just gross." Kali lowered the teen gently onto the cushions. She ripped at the tattered sleeve of Soriya's shirt to expose the wound.

"What happened to her?"

The stab from the demon blade pulsed in black. It looked like decayed flesh, spreading out in all directions. Tendrils thickened with each breath. Soriya needed the oxygen, but at the same time all it did was accelerate her injury.

"She's been infected."

"There's a hospital down the street." Urg towered over them from behind the couch. He blocked the light. Kali swatted him aside for a better view of her patient.

"Like they'd have a damn clue." This was her fault. She should have done more to keep Soriya out of the line of fire. Going to the prison had been yet another bad decision in a long night of them.

"Hey." Urg grabbed Kali's shoulder and pulled her back. "Tell me what the hell is going on."

Kali ran her hands over her face, then settled along the edge of the coffee table. "She asked for you, all right? We needed a safe place. Caldwell was swarming with cops, and I didn't have time for twenty questions, all of which would have ended with us behind bars."

"Caldwell?" Urg asked, his concern growing by the second. "There was a massacre there. The news is saying an entire cellblock was killed. How did you survive?"

"We got lucky," Kali muttered. "Sort of."

Soriya screamed. The blackness around her wound had finally snaked its way through her entire body. Kali could see waves running down her legs and up her arms. The pain had clearly increased and the infection was about to reach its terminal point. There was no more time for discussion. Kali had to act. She had to try and do something for the girl who had risked everything to stop Shiva.

"Hold her still," Kali ordered the orc. Urg shifted to the end of the couch, but hesitated to touch the spasming Soriya. "I said, hold her!"

Urg clamped down on Soriya, locking her down against the cushions. Kali pushed the coffee table out of her way and leaned close. The wound reeked of the dead and the dying. Worse, Kali could feel the darkness inside Soriya. It drew her closer with each whiff.

"What are you doing?" Urg asked.

Kali tucked her hair away, her lips inches from the pulsing

wound. "Soriya's been struck with the demon blade. It's sent a powerful poison into her system that will eventually overpower and kill her."

"A poison? What kind of poison could do this?"

"Sin."

Urg eased his hold, which allowed Soriya's arms to swing out. Kali fell back to avoid the blow. Urg quickly regained his composure and applied more pressure to keep the patient in position.

"Sin?"

"Pure sin," Kali said. "I need to get it out of her now."

"How?" Urg asked. Kali answered by putting her lips to the puncture wound. "Wait!"

She ignored him and focused. With every ounce of will she drew the poison into her, sucking on the darkness that filled Soriya's dying body. After her first enormous intake, Kali noticed the black threads recede along Soriya's chest and arms. She continued until there was nothing dotting the girl's skin and only the puncture wound remained.

Soriya sat up, the force surprising both Urg and Kali. Both reeled from the sudden movement. Soriya's eyes opened. She cried out from the shock of the procedure. Then she collapsed and fell unconscious once again.

Kali kept her hand over her mouth, her cheeks puffed out to contain the darkness. Urg wiped at his brow.

"The blackness..." he started, looking over Soriya with care. "It's gone. You did it. You—"

Kali jumped to her feet. She ran across the room and down the hall. The bathroom door slammed open, and she dropped in front of the toilet. Raising the lid, she expelled everything she had drawn into her. Every ounce of the darkness spewed into the bowl in a series of massive heaves. After each one, Kali flushed, letting the rushing water swallow the darkness.

A sigh of relief escaped her when she was through. She lay alongside the toilet, her body physically exhausted from the violent act.

Urg stood in the doorway, hands to his hips. "You okay?"

Kali wiped spittle that ran down her chin. "I am now. Can't

have that stuff in me. Not a drop. Too risky."

"Considering what it did to Soriya, I believe it," Urg said with a nod. He tilted his head to the living room and the resting teen. "Will she be okay?"

Kali offered a slight nod, but remained silent. She lifted herself from the floor, then started out of the room. Urg stepped aside to give her a clear path to the living room. She stopped short of the couch. Soriya's eyes shifted beneath her lids, a fitful sleep taking hold.

"You should let her rest as long as possible," Kali said. She moved for the door.

"What about you?" Urg asked. "Where are you going?"

"I…" Kali took a breath. Soriya had fought the fight meant for Kali, and paid the price for it. Everything Kali had done was for self-preservation. That was not what Soriya needed at her side. She needed a friend, someone willing to look out for her well-being. Kali had only looked out for herself. It was all she knew how to do. "I'm no nursemaid. There's nothing else I can do for her."

"Hey," Urg said, stopping her at the door. "You're supposed to be Soriya's friend."

"No," Kali replied. "That's the *last* thing I am to her."

She had used Soriya, coerced her into a fight she had no chance of winning. That wasn't what a friend did. Soriya never should have stuck with her. She sure as hell never should have taken Kali's hand in that alley outside the animal shelter.

"Sorry," Kali said. "I have to go."

She shut the door behind her, refusing to listen to another word from Urg. Kali's hands trembled. Small steps carried her to the stairs at the end of the hall. It was better for her to go, better for everyone involved. She had only brought Soriya pain and disappointment.

There was nothing more she could do for the kid. Nothing more she could do for anyone now. She'd had her chance at the prison. If she had stood up and faced her demons things might have been different. Instead, she had stayed silent and cowered out of fear. It was better for everyone involved if she walked away. The end was coming anyway.

Nothing would stand in Shiva's way now.

CHAPTER TWENTY-EIGHT

Panic set in the second he hung up the phone. By the time Ruiz reached Mercy Hospital at the heart of downtown Portents, he was manic. Sweat dribbled down his palms and across his face. The world passed by in a blur of color. Street lights left orange streaks across his field of vision. The overhead fluorescents burned brighter than the sun. People stared in his direction, off-kilter looks of concern, but no one said anything. No one helped him. No one saw the desperation in his eyes or in each hurried step. They had their own concerns and couldn't be bothered, it seemed.

If only they knew what he did, what he had seen in that temple… the threat that hid in Portents. People were dying and the police did everything they could to calm the fears of the populace. Ruiz was doing everything he could to calm his own.

By the time he reached the nurse's station, his throat was dry and his chest was heaving. A young woman with a pale complexion cocked an eyebrow at his approach, then cast a look to anyone in her vicinity as if begging for help. No one was close enough to intercept Ruiz.

"My… my wife!" he shouted, waving cool air in his face. "I'm here to see…"

"Take a breath, sir," the nurse said. She stood and circled the desk.

Ruiz fought against his breast pocket, which seemed like an impenetrable lock. At last, his badge fell out on the counter. Security looked on with growing concern from the other side of the hall. Ruiz lifted the badge and held it in front of nurse's face.

"Captain," he said. He coughed hard to clear his throat, then offered an awkward smile. "Ruiz. I'm here for—"

"Michelle Ruiz," the nurse finished. She then nodded, awareness in her face, like everything suddenly made sense about him. "Right this way."

He followed the nurse down the hall. His steps were hurried, and he had to force himself to slow his pace as they went. Ruiz dabbed at his forehead with his sleeve, while wiping his hand on the inside of the cuff. Nothing helped.

"That bad, huh?" he asked.

The nurse glanced at him, curious. "Excuse me?"

"You recognized the name."

"I admitted your wife," she replied, though she couldn't make eye contact with him. She kept her head low as they rounded the corner deeper into the maternity ward.

Ruiz nodded in understanding. "I'm sorry you had to deal with that."

The nurse smiled. "I've actually never heard that many vulgarities strung together in a single sentence."

"It's a gift," Ruiz said with a sigh.

"I don't think they were necessary."

"She thinks differently," he said. "Or the baby does. I'm not sure which would be worse."

Michelle had never been the calmest pregnant woman on the planet. The only reason he had managed to avoid her wrath when he left for work was because of the late hour. Had she had an ounce of energy left in her there would have been blood spilled in the kitchen. Ruiz had no doubt about that. Somehow he loved that about her, her heart, her fire. It was like she could take on the world if you threatened her family.

It was the way he'd always wanted to be too. Work, however, always seemed to get in the way. The job meant sacrifice and his family had been the one to pay the price. This time was supposed to be different. This time he was supposed to be there with Michelle for the birth. He couldn't be too late. He couldn't break another promise.

The nurse stopped short of the delivery ward. "This is where—"

"Alejo!" Michelle screamed from the far end of the hall. She lay on a bed, breathing heavy and holding her stomach as she was wheeled toward the delivery room. "Get your ass over here! Now!"

The nurse took a step back and patted his shoulder. "I think you're all set."

Ruiz mouthed a silent apology, then nodded. "Thank you."

"No need," she said as she left with a wave. "That's what the bill is for."

Ruiz broke into a run to close the gap as attendants continued their walk to the delivery room at the end of the corridor. They entered, and the doors flapped closed in Ruiz's face. He immediately pushed them open to be with his wife.

"Michelle. Are you—?"

"I'm—"

The doctor, a man in his twenties from the looks of him, cut between them. He was all scrubbed up with a mask hiding his baby face. "Right on time, sir. Your wife is ready to get this show on the road."

"I've been ready for *weeks*," Michelle seethed between breaths. "Weeks! Tell him!"

His wife glared at him with dangerous eyes. He turned to the doctor. "It's been weeks."

The attendants moved Michelle's bed into the center of the room. Nurses positioned monitors to check on her levels, and then scribbled notes on required forms. Ruiz took a moment to lean closer to the doctor.

"Nothing for the pain?"

The doctor motioned for a nurse and took the chart. He scanned it quickly. "She's had the epidural already."

"Christ," Ruiz whispered, then offered the sign of the cross. He hadn't been through this with her. He had been working, always buried in a case. How had he not been here with her before? How could he make his wife go through this a third time? The better question might have been why had she agreed.

"Prayer will only take us so far," the doctor said with a wink. He ushered Ruiz back to his wife's side. "We're all set."

"How is everything looking?" Ruiz asked. His nerves compounded with each angry breath from his wife. "Is the baby—?"

"Everything's good," the doctor answered. "Isn't that right, Michelle?"

"Get this baby out of me now!" she howled, hands clenched tight to the sides of the bed.

Ruiz gulped. "Can I wait outside?"

"Alejo!"

He moved closer to his wife. A homicidal god of destruction in the city was starting to sound pretty good to him.

"Michelle," the doctor called. "I need you ready to push."

Michelle growled in frustration. She had been ready to push for over a month—Ruiz knew she didn't need any more directions. What she needed was for this to be over.

"Sir?" a nurse said, hand to Ruiz's arm. "Please take your wife's hand."

He hesitated before complying. When he finally clasped her hand in his, it brought a smile to Michelle's face, even through the thick layer of sweat covering her skin.

"You made it," she said. Her anger melted away.

"I promised."

"I didn't think you would. I thought…" Tears streamed down her cheeks. "Oh, God, and now I'm crying."

A contraction ended the sobbing, and Michelle let out an involuntary scream of pain. She squeezed Ruiz's hand and his eyes began to water from the pressure.

"Me too," he said under his breath.

She pulled him closer. "I love you. I love our family."

"I love you. You're doing great."

"Need that push now," the doctor said. He looked up at them and winked again. Ruiz was starting to hate that wink.

Michelle screamed and Ruiz joined her. This was the moment he had prepared for ever since he found out they were expecting. He had made a promise and kept it. This was their moment, for their family.

This was where he belonged—where he always belonged.

CHAPTER TWENTY-NINE

Soriya's eyes snapped open. She jolted upright and immediately felt pain course through her body. Every muscle ached, every bone hurt. Lying back down did nothing to assist Soriya's discomfort. She tried to sit up and found a pair of coarse hands along her back.

"Easy," Urg said. "Easy, now."

His presence nearly made her jump again, but she fought to control her reaction. She eased along the side of the couch, aided by the hulking orc.

"What happened?" she asked. Daylight peeked through the blinds along the window. The neon lights of the apartment complex, which was her usual view from her friend's apartment, were turned off. Instead of the dull hum from the sign, she heard the traffic of midday rushing along the corridors of Portents. "How long have I—?"

"Questions later," Urg interrupted. He circled the couch and lifted up a steaming cup from the table. "Tea first."

Soriya sank into the cushion. Her body screamed for a relief she could not provide. She took hold of the cup. The porcelain burned at the touch, thanks to the blisters along her fingers. Steam rose up and she allowed the scent to waft beneath her nose. "Tea?"

"A nice chamomile."

She cocked an eyebrow at him and threw him a thin smirk.

Urg rolled his eyes at her reaction. "Don't give me that look. You almost ended up with a lamb's-blood mixture my mother taught me as a kid. Great home remedy for purging toxins, but you humans are so unpredictable. Wasn't sure how you would react."

Soriya smiled and lifted the cup. "I appreciate the effort."

She took a long sip. The tea burned on the way down. She did her best to keep it down, the taste nothing like the chamomile Mentor provided at home. When she had finished, Soriya raised her hand toward Urg.

"Help me up?"

Urg grumbled, "Or you could sit and drink your damn tea."

When she refused to comply, he took her waiting hand and pulled her to her feet. She was careful to keep the tea upright, though if some spilled it was for the best. Her legs threatened to give out at first. Thankfully, though, the pain lessened with each movement. Her body was stiff and needed to be free from the couch.

Urg shook his head. "Yeah, why bother listening to me? Teenagers. Worse than Carpathian bloodspawn."

Soriya grinned. "You're showing your age again, Urg."

"You are as well."

She ignored the comment as best as she could. Soriya had heard enough about her youth from people. Everyone knew better than her, everyone saw the world more clearly, and everyone understood her role in it while she remained clueless. That was their perception and she was tired of it. She needed to be in charge of her own destiny for a change, one she thought she had always known.

Until Kali. Until Shiva.

Soriya rubbed at the wound on her shoulder. The darkness was gone. All that remained was an open puncture wound, but even that appeared small and inconsequential. How had she healed so quickly?

Soriya lowered her tea along the window sill. She opened the blinds and stared out at the corridor between buildings that ran the length of the block. "Where is she, Urg?"

"She left."

Her head bowed slightly and her shoulders slumped forward. "Of course she did."

Kali would never be the type to stick around. She had no intention of being there in Soriya's time of need. Hell, she hadn't even lifted a finger to stop Shiva at Caldwell. Every act taken had been under duress, or for her own self-interest. Standing up to Shiva meant facing her fears. That wasn't Kali at all. If it wasn't fun it didn't matter to her.

"Soriya?" Urg called, ending her rumination. Soriya moved from the window, arms across her chest.

"She stood by and did nothing," she said. "Kali would rather drink herself into a stupor than put up a fight. She's so concerned about herself that she'd let Portents suffer."

Frustrated, she returned to the view outside. She lifted the tea and took another sip, though the beverage did nothing to soothe her. The cup rattled against the saucer when she set it back down.

"I thought... I *hoped* it would be different with her. That she would be someone I could talk to, someone to help deal with the insanity that comes with the Greystone. I really thought she could take away some of the burden. Maybe be a friend. That's not Kali though, is it?"

Urg moved to her side. "The burden is different for us all, Soriya. The responsibility you feel is your own. Kali takes hers and channels it to laugh at life. You focus yours on the stone and your work. Instead of forcing Kali to see your point of view you should try and see hers."

"Portents—"

"Will always be threatened," Urg said. He lifted her gaze to meet his and smiled at her. "Portents will always find a way to endure. I'm only asking you to try, Soriya."

Soriya shook her head. She stepped away from the window and paced the length of the room. "How? She left."

"She didn't go far," Urg answered. He peered up at the ceiling. "Kali's been on the roof all day."

"How do you—?"

Urg laughed. "I never told you about an orc's hearing? I could detect a muslipin in her cave from a hundred yards out."

"I don't have a clue what you just said," Soriya remarked.

"Muslipins? They're these little rat things that eat—"

"Sorry," she said with a wave to stop him. "What I meant

was, thanks for putting up with me, Urg."

"Always."

Soriya started for the door.

"Hold it," Urg said. She stopped with a huff.

"What now?"

He held out the cup to her. "Finish your tea."

"It's terrible."

Urg sighed. "I know. Lamb's blood next time." He took it to the kitchen and dumped the beverage. Then he opened the fridge and removed a small plate. "Maybe this will work better for you."

"What did you do?" Sitting on the plate was a single cupcake. Urg grabbed a small candle and set it on top. He lit the candle and handed her the treat. "Urg…"

"It's store bought," Urg reassured her with a grin. "So blow out the candle and make a damn wish already."

CHAPTER THIRTY

He didn't want to be there. Mentor took his place inside the four pillars that locked the Bypass in the cavernous chamber beneath the city. Every time he looked at the floating orb the question returned. As it passed his thoughts the Bypass illuminated. The green hue of the surface darkened and small black flits of light spun rapidly along the surface. Within the black were two small specks of color—one red and one blue.

They were the eyes of the man who would one day kill him.

No, Mentor thought as he shook his head. The image dissipated along the surface. *Not now. That's not why I'm here.*

Shiva was out there. The god of destruction, a force of nature, was loose in Portents and they had no idea where he could be. Mentor had not heard from Soriya in hours. Something had happened at the prison just outside the city. The situation had concluded before Mentor could even get there. He had been clear on the other side of Portents when it occurred.

Part of him knew Soriya had played a role in the prison massacre. She had always flocked to danger, always struggled to play it safe when lives were on the line. If Kali was to be believed, everyone on the planet was at risk with Shiva's presence. He was a deity with the power to end all life. He was never meant to return to the realm of the living, never meant to stand side by side with mankind.

Mentor feared for his student. He continued to worry even after promising to rein in his concerns following the Minotaur's rampage months earlier. It was difficult, to say the least. He tried to focus on her strengths, to recognize the skills she had acquired thanks to his constant lessons. But Shiva was on another level. No one could prepare for him. No one could face him head to head.

They had to try, though. He knew Soriya especially had to try. It was in her nature.

She would be fine. That thought carried him back to the chamber and the task ahead: to find Shiva before anything else happened.

Mentor placed the stone before him. Deep, cleansing breaths wiped the concern and the doubts from his mind. He closed his eyes and prepared.

"Where is he?"

The Bypass replied, drawing Mentor beyond the veil. His essence soared through the crossroads locked inside the floating orb of light. Around him all of time and space opened up. Screams echoed from the depths, his own and those of the damned lost to the ages.

Mentor ignored them. This wasn't about him. It couldn't be about his failures to come or the nightmare of leaving Soriya to fend for herself. She would be fine, but only if they stopped Shiva from destroying everything they sought to protect.

Shifting images splintered and Mentor landed along the surface of a street. He recognized the skyline of downtown to his left. There were no structures immediately off the side of the road. Four lanes stretched in each direction with cones dotting half the road. One lane was ripped apart completely.

Sitting in the center median was Shiva. He carried a blade of obsidian. Mentor tried to reach for it, but was locked in place. He could not interact within the Bypass. He could only listen and learn. Any movement too far into the void resulted in losing access to his body. In the past, he had pushed the limits and almost became a wraith in the infinite as a result. He understood the Bypass better now.

He decided to simply watch the scene unfold. Shiva lifted the blade by the handle and the darkness of the steel flowed into him. Once-blue skin was overtaken by shadow and swallowed whole.

The shadow continued to grow.

Mentor cried out at the darkness, but the sound was lost. The shadow loomed taller and taller with each moment. It spread across the eight-lane highway and rushed toward him. In the darkness, for the briefest of instants, Mentor saw a face form and a large smile widen.

Then it was over. Mentor opened his eyes to find the Bypass before him and his Greystone at his feet. The vision had ended, but every impression remained carved into his soul. He felt chilled by the experience—more nervous than ever at their chances of success.

None of that mattered, however. Not now. He had entered the infinite void of the Bypass for one reason and one reason alone: to learn the whereabouts of Shiva. Mentor stood and slipped the Greystone back into the pouch at his hip. He knew where he had to go.

CHAPTER THIRTY-ONE

Soriya hesitated at the rooftop door. She should have immediately started her search the moment she woke up. Shiva was loose in the city, threatening the lives of everyone, yet she couldn't help herself. She had to see Kali one last time.

Picking at the scraps of frosting at the corner of her mouth, Soriya turned the handle. The door opened silently and daylight poured into the stairwell. Spring struggled to reclaim the city from the long winter. The air was cool, but the sun felt refreshing instead of the typical winter gloom that had seized control of Portents for months.

Kali sat on the ledge. Her feet dangled over the side, kicking at the air. Strands of her hair whipped in the wind. She didn't appear to be an immortal goddess. She wasn't a figure of death or a powerful deity. Kali was merely human, vulnerable to the ways of the world like everyone else.

When the door connected with the side of the building, Kali peered toward the new arrival. Sullen eyes grew wide and the joyful exuberance she displayed at their first meeting returned in an instant.

"There she is," Kali announced. She spun back toward the building, then jumped to her feet. "It worked. Let me see."

Kali reached for Soriya's shoulder, but the young teen pulled away. The jerking motion caused pain to shoot down her right side from the freshly healed wound. Soriya shifted into the openness of the rooftop and turned her back to the concerned woman.

"I'm fine."

"Hey," Kali said. "No sour grapes, Soriya. I saved your life."

Soriya swallowed her anger, though it ran red hot through her body. Her fists clenched and every muscle in her body tightened.

"What is it, kid?" Kali pressed.

"How do I stop him?" Soriya asked. She stared out toward the city. The sun slowly faded between skyscrapers.

"What?" The question staggered Kali. "You can't be serious."

"I am, Kali," Soriya replied, resolute in her determination. "How do I stop Shiva?"

"You almost died!" Kali shouted. There was no irritation behind it and no frustration, only concern. But Soriya no longer knew if it was for her or if it was only for Kali herself. "We barely escaped with our lives and *that's* the question you lead with?"

"It's the only one that matters."

Kali shook her head. "Not even close. You matter. I matter. All this matters!" She stepped back to the ledge, hands spread wide to highlight the bustle of activity in Portents. Horns blared from rushing cars below them on the street. Televisions buzzed from inside the apartments and across the way in storefront windows. The mutters of pedestrians rose up to fill the air. It all brought a smile to Kali's lips. Soriya didn't share it with her. "Enjoy the day, Soriya. Forget about this whole thing. Please. Come with me and we'll get a drink. We'll be free."

"Stop," Soriya snapped. She wanted to lash out. She wanted to scream. How could Kali not want to help? It ate away at Soriya. Her hands were squeezed into fists as she tried to focus and contain her rage. "Just stop. I've had enough of your speeches. All the games and the distractions. You could have ended this at the prison. You didn't. Why?"

"Dammit, Soriya. This isn't—"

"The truth, Kali," Soriya said. "Now."

"Because I'll die!" Kali bellowed. Tear-filled eyes screamed at Soriya for understanding. "All right? You happy?"

Soriya didn't know what to say. She didn't know how to respond. Nothing about their time together brought to light what

Kali had been hiding. She had lived in the moment, taking joy with every act. That was all she wanted. Yet, there had been moments of pure fear in Kali's eyes. Soriya recalled Kali's apprehension at the bar as she looked around for signs of trouble. Then there was her dread when it came to Shiva. Kali had refused to help at every opportunity. She had pushed Soriya to walk away rather than confront the danger Shiva posed. Now Soriya realized why. Because Kali knew that her life of fun and frivolity would end and she would be forced to finally face the truth.

"That's *my* fate," Kali continued. She turned away from Soriya, settling back to the ledge. Her hands gripped tight to the brick at her sides. Tears ran down her cheeks and dripped to the pavement below. "That's my destiny in this godforsaken world. Shiva unleashes the Raktabija and I am forced to stop it. But I die in the process." She swiped at her eyes. "No, not even die. It's worse than death. I become another aspect, a different person completely. This, who I am, will be erased and overwritten. Like I never existed. Like I never mattered in the first place."

It was where her fear had come from, the terror that followed her with every stray glance at the bar or the silence that answered every question asked. Kali had held it all back. She'd fought against a fate that would damn her in the end.

Soriya sat at her side. Her hand fell on top of Kali's and she squeezed it. "Kali, I didn't—"

A sad smile spread on her face. "I know, right? The goddess of death and destruction afraid of her own mortality. Pretty hilarious, isn't it?"

"Hey," Soriya said. Kali refused to look at her directly. Instead, she focused on the rising noise of the city and the darkening skyline in the distance. "I... I understand, Kali. Death is something I've always had to consider. It's always in the back of my mind. It has been since I lost my parents. I don't want to die. But *someone* has to face the darkness. Someone has to do the right thing no matter the outcome. That's what I'm going to do, Kali. Help me do the right thing."

For a moment, Soriya almost believed her words had been enough. A nod escaped Kali. It was as if she finally understood the true stakes of the situation. That she accepted her destiny and put everyone else first.

Kali shook free from Soriya's hand and stood. Her eyes went cold. "I can't, Soriya. I can't risk facing him again."

This time it was Soriya who nodded. She did understand, though it pained her to admit. Fate was funny that way. Knowing it made people either work harder to reach their destiny or run that much farther in the opposite direction. Kali would never stop running—she couldn't. She was too afraid. There was none of the strength Soriya had witnessed the previous night with the Tengu. None of the attitude that had drawn them together in the first place.

There was only the terror of losing what little Kali truly had.

"Okay," Soriya said. She made her way to her feet. Time grew short and she had things to do. She had to find Shiva. Even more importantly, she had to find a way to stop him—no matter what anyone said.

"Soriya, wait," Kali called after her. Soriya hesitated at the door, then let go of the handle. She faced the goddess once more. As Kali approached, she untied the ribbon at her wrist. The strands whipped wildly around her, fighting against their owner. Kali held out the mysterious item. "Here. A gift."

Soriya took the ribbon in hand, confused. "I... I don't—"

Kali closed it in her grip. The strands settled as if understanding who they now belonged to in some way. "The ribbon is a piece of me," she said. "My essence and my spirit. It will strive to protect you with every strand of its being."

Soriya tied the end of the pink ribbon to her left bicep. The strands snaked their way down her arm in a braided pattern. "Yeah, but how does it look?"

"Great, kid," Kali said. "Really great."

Soriya hitched her thumb toward the door. "I should get moving."

Halfway into the darkness of the stairwell, she heard Kali's voice once more. "He'll need space." Kali was at the landing, gaze lost to the shadows. "To unleash the Raktabija he'll need to go somewhere no one else will be around to interrupt. Somewhere he can take his time and get the details right."

It wasn't a definitive answer, but it was a start. "Thank you, Kali. For the gift. And for saving my life."

"I wish I could do more," she said. "I won't, but the desire is there."

"If only that were enough."

Soriya headed toward the darkness and the night ahead. She left Kali alone on the rooftop to consider both her choices and the consequences they wrought.

CHAPTER THIRTY-TWO

The apartment was vacant. No lights illuminated the space. The dull hum of the refrigerator accompanied Soriya's steps from the kitchen to the living room. The coffee table was clear of items. It was a definite departure from her last visit to the home of Bethany Schmidt—now Bethany Loren.

Why did I come here? The question followed her. It begged for an answer, but the teen had none to give. She found herself at the fire escape on instinct alone. The lock made little difference to her. She had found it easy to circumnavigate whenever she felt the need to visit her friend.

Was that the reason behind her visit? Had she needed a friend, someone who truly understood what was happening in Portents? Soriya had hoped Kali could have been that person. She had been a fighter in Soriya's eyes, knowledgeable yet also able to stand against the growing darkness that seemed unending in the city.

Beth had helped Soriya when the Minotaur found his way out of the labyrinth. The woman had offered advice and stood by Soriya's side when the battle occurred. She hadn't run scared and terrified of the possible outcome. Beth had proved to be far more of a warrior than Kali.

The truth was, Soriya needed her again. Kali had set her on the path to find Shiva, but the frightened goddess had left too much to chance with not enough time to seek out every wide open space unpopulated within the city limits. There were too many options, and she worried that every tick of the clock might signal the end for everyone.

Those were the stakes, and they weighed down Soriya with each thought. It wasn't a case of a monster with a straightforward target. It was about everything she loved and everyone she held dear. Part of her stopped to warn Beth, while another part had hoped she could provide Soriya with the confidence to fight on and stand as she always had.

When did things get so complicated?

Soriya leaned against the mantel. Along the center, before the mirror, sat a photo from Beth's wedding day. There was pure joy in Beth's smile over being wed to the man she loved more than anything. It gave Soriya pause, her eyes sullen. Beth didn't need the burden of Soriya's task. She had her own happiness, her own life to contend with. This was for Soriya and for her alone, much as it pained her to admit.

Doubt remained. Beth had questioned her youth when they met. Kali had done the same in her own unique way. Maybe their questions were valid. Maybe they knew her better than she knew herself. Hell, everyone seemed so sure about Soriya's path. What if fate had intended something else for her? What if Shiva wasn't the end, but a new beginning?

Soriya groaned with frustration. She slammed her hands against her thighs and paced the length of the room. After collapsing along the edge of the couch, she smothered her face into a pillow and screamed. Every doubt, every ounce of anger and rage filled the fabric until she ran out of breath.

"What if all I want is to celebrate my birthday? Is that so wrong?"

It had been a mistake to come. She had known about Beth's honeymoon plans for weeks. They had talked about it over breakfast one morning after Beth's daily jog. Soriya had joked about staying in the city for the trip, to which Beth laughed uncontrollably.

Soriya was glad Beth was gone now. Her friend was away from the terror of Shiva's arrival and the pain to come. She couldn't have faced Beth, not with the doubts and the regrets that ate at her worse than the stab wound from the demon blade.

She had to find a way to locate Shiva. She had to stop him,

and every second in the vacant apartment wasted another opportunity. There had to be a way.

Standing to leave, Soriya moved for the kitchen. In the doorway was Mentor, gray eyes beaming through the darkness of the home.

"I had a feeling you would be here."

"Mentor?" His presence surprised her. She wiped at watery eyes before drying her hands along her pants. "What are you doing here?"

Mentor paced the room, surveying the contents of the apartment from the television to the coat rack in the corner. All appeared normal and mundane, which were words they'd never use to describe their living quarters.

"She's been a good friend to you," Mentor said. He paused at the mantel and the image of Beth smiling. "She listened when you needed an ear. I'm sorry I haven't always been—"

"You have," Soriya said, cutting him off. He was right though. She should have turned to him first. After talking with Kali however, she couldn't. She was too embarrassed to explain the truth behind her doubts. "It's different with Beth. A different perspective."

Mentor nodded. "I'm here now."

"I know," Soriya said, tilting her head toward the exit. "But it's nothing. Really. I shouldn't have—"

"Soriya," Mentor said, approaching her. His hands fell on her shoulders and he pulled her close in an embrace. "Tell me."

She squeezed him tight, then stepped back. She picked at the ribbon along her left arm. "Is this really what I'm meant for? Am I merely denying all other possibilities for nothing more than a dream?"

"Ah," Mentor said. He read her wavering gaze. "This is about Kali."

"Yes... No." Soriya stopped and groaned with frustration. "It's just that I've always wanted this. To fight the monsters. To be the Greystone."

"What if there's more?" he finished for her.

"More like, what if I'm supposed to be doing something else instead? What if I'm not the best choice for the Greystone because of that?"

Mentor ushered her to the couch, and once there she fell against the cushion. Mentor joined her, though he didn't look directly at her. He leaned against his knees and stared at the emptiness of the apartment. "Kali denies her fate out of fear. You embrace your path through will and determination."

"Because of you," Soriya said. "Maybe it's always been you and never me. In any of this."

"Do you honestly believe that?"

"I don't know." She closed her eyes. She didn't want to think about it anymore. She didn't want to face the tough questions, because the answers never came easily for her. In the darkness of her thoughts, though, came something else entirely.

It came in the remembrance of better days in the Bypass chamber. It came in the lessons learned and the battles—both physical and mental—that had changed her from a child to a warrior. Through them Soriya had found purpose and light. Her memory raised her up instead of weighed her down.

When she opened her eyes, Mentor was before her. He took her hands in his, and she saw a fatherly look in his eyes. "Soriya," he started, his voice thunderous in the silence of the home. "This choice has to be yours. No one holds you in place. No one forces your hand. Not me. Not Kali. Only you. I won't stop you, whatever your decision."

It was her choice. It had always been her choice. With his words came that simple truth. When he had offered her an escape from the orphanage and set her on the path, he'd done so only as a guide. He had made the offer, but she had taken the first step and every one since.

The decision had always been hers to live free or accept a great responsibility—to walk away or stand up for something. She had decided to protect Portents as the Greystone.

She nodded, finally understanding. "I made my choice a long time ago."

Mentor smiled. "Good. Now how about we kick some ass, and then grab a pizza?"

"That's the best offer I've had all day."

He helped her to her feet and the pair started for the fire escape and the fight of their lives.

CHAPTER THIRTY-THREE

The expressway project had started with an exercise in futility. The budget had never sat right with the council members, and the public hated every last aspect of it, but the city workers union had pushed for the construction during weighty contract negotiations and won. Crews had broken ground as soon as the snow stopped flying, though the cold temperatures had made any progress negligible.

Estimates put the project at two years in length, but knowing the way the city typically operated, and with budgetary issues blocking overtime shifts at night and on the weekends, that term would most likely stretch to three or four years by the end. Entrances to the thoroughfare were closed from the edge of Lowtown all the way through the Knoll and downtown districts. Dozens of miles of road were blocked from the thousands of commuters that clogged the city during the morning hours.

It was a nightmare for most. City workers, however, cheered for the job ahead. They coned off multiple entry points, tore up entire lanes of the road, and made a giant mess of the six-mile stretch of expressway under their control. Equipment had been stationed along the sides, trucks were parked every which way, and portable toilets had been positioned in tune with the mile markers for easy access.

They toiled during the daylight hours to show the city they were getting the job done, amid the screams of the populace on every news channel and daily publication. When the sun waned and the shifts ended, though, the expressway emptied of life. The RDJ had once been called the only major artery in the city, serving people from every suburb and province as they scurried to the heart of Portents for work and entertainment. Every other roadway had been nothing more than blood vessels feeding the smaller districts. Now, the RDJ was lifeless—a dead zone in Portents.

Its emptiness served the purposes of another.

Mentor led his student up the on-ramp off South Allen. He explained his reasoning to Soriya as they journeyed from Beth's apartment. Her concern grew as he relayed his trip through the Bypass for answers. He didn't dare to make the attempt unless it was absolutely necessary and had always kept her away for fear of losing control during a vital search. Her own knowledge of Shiva's needs, thanks to Kali's advice, had cemented their destination.

They walked side by side. They were a team in the endeavor. It had been a long time in the making. For years, he had shielded her from the life. Since the Minotaur attack, he had eased off on the parental limitations of their work and allowed her to explore the role she would eventually take over. It was tough, to say the least. His concerns followed him no matter what the situation, and his fear for her life weighed heavily on his decisions. He had tried to move past them, however, to accept the future as it was—no matter how the story ended.

It felt right having her at his side: as natural as breathing. Teaching had brought them together, but lessons could only carry them so far. The fight ahead, taking the challenge to Shiva directly as a pair, meant the world to him.

When they reached the expressway, they paused. The lights continued to operate along the road, as they were still timed to illuminate the area during the night hours. They were staggered on both sides, one side bright while the other was lost to shadow and vice versa.

In the distance, before a row of construction vehicles parked for the night, they found him waiting. Shiva sat with his legs crossed and his eyes closed. His blue skin practically glowed. Resting on his palms was the demon blade. The darkness of the steel pulsed with energy. His body never touched the ground. He floated two feet from the pavement, his lips muttering unknown words in meditation.

Soriya made the first move and Mentor followed. His step was awkward as he tried to keep up with his ward. Pain shot from his knee and he staggered slightly. His injury was getting worse.

Soriya paused when she noticed his struggle. "You sure you're up for this?"

When she reached for him, he waved her off. He steadied his balance and they continued their approach. He beamed at her strength and her resolve. No matter the doubts and the frustrations, somehow Soriya always found a way to stand and fight. She was always there, not only for him but for the city. And she would be, long after he was gone. She was a far better Greystone than he'd ever been, even at such a young age.

"Try to keep up, little one," he said.

Their hands stayed close to the hand-woven pouches along their hips. The ribbon running down Soriya's left arm whipped through the air at her side, though never in concert with the wind swirling down the road. It suited her in some way: like a missing piece that completed the puzzle.

"What is he doing?" Soriya asked as they closed the gap.

"Preparing," Mentor answered.

"He's about to summon the Raktabija," Soriya said. She raced ahead in a charge. "Can't have that."

"Soriya, wait—"

"Shiva!" she called, stopping short of his presence. Mentor joined her.

The god opened his eyes. Both glowed in white. Power coursed through him. His feet touched the ground as he grasped the hilt of the demon blade.

"Ah, the protector returns," Shiva said. Excitement spread across his face. "With a guardian in tow, no less."

"This ends here, Shiva," Mentor said, causing Soriya to glance at him. There was no fear in her eyes. No doubt. She stood ready to face the threat, no matter the outcome. He could do no less.

Shiva pointed his sword at them. "Very well. Try and fight the storm to come."

CHAPTER THIRTY-FOUR

They attacked as one. One look was all it took to put them on the same page. Soriya led; it was her way and always would be. She drove forward hard with her fist. Shiva, of course, read the blow immediately and sidestepped.

Right into the waiting Mentor.

A strong left slammed Shiva back, but he never lost his balance. Not that they wanted him to, as Soriya was in position to follow up with a kick that knocked out his legs. Shiva fell to the pavement, but flipped away to avoid the next attack.

Soriya shared a smirk with her teacher. They had spent over a decade preparing for a fight like this. Every move had been achieved through lessons learned and battles won. She may have cursed the ten-hour sessions in the Bypass chamber practicing the same precision strike against the dummies Mentor had positioned around the room, but it had all been worth it.

Mentor advanced on their target. Shiva assumed Soriya would be the aggressor and held the demon blade to defend against her assault. Mentor, however, was able to skirt the danger of the obsidian instrument with a kick to Shiva's right side.

The hit caused the flailing deity to lower his blade, which Soriya took as her signal. She leapt at him, pouncing on him like a cat, to drive him back to the ground. Shiva's arm slammed into her shoulder, which still wasn't back to a hundred percent after her stabbing. Soriya cried out and fell away. Before she could find her balance again, Shiva was on his feet, ready for the next round.

Mentor covered for her as she rebounded from the blow.

She took a step back, stretching out her arm to work out the pain from her wound. As she did, she marveled at her teacher. He moved like lightning, as if the pain in his knee had never been there. When she was a child she'd never been allowed to be privy to the myths he hunted. The cases he solved were stories to tell around the fireplace in the Bypass. The way he anticipated Shiva's movements, the way he never faltered between strikes—always one step ahead—amazed her.

How could I have ever wanted to do anything different?

Her indecision and doubt faded away like a bad memory. In its place was the resolve Mentor had taught her so long ago. It was the strength she always carried in defiance of the monsters plaguing Portents. This was where she belonged. This was where she'd always wanted to be, the path that had been started the moment she found the stone beneath the burning wreckage of her old life. She never wanted to be anything else, nor did she want to do anything else with her life. This was her purpose, her fate, and her destiny.

She jumped back into the battle with a fire in her eyes.

"You fight in vain," Shiva said as he defended against their combined assault. "What I offer is a cleansing, a renewal for this world. No more sin. No more darkness. Those that remain will be pure. Just like you, protector."

Mentor's punch missed and Shiva kicked him in the back. The aging teacher fell forward and hit the pavement. His leg bent awkwardly as he crashed onto the concrete.

"Mentor!" Soriya dove to help and Shiva caught her by the arm. He yanked her close, then grabbed her by the throat.

"Let her go," Mentor said. He struggled to right himself, holding a hand to his faulty knee.

Shiva refused, and his white eyes gleamed over the fallen teacher. "*She* is pure. But you? I see so many hidden things buried inside you. Secrets devour us over time, guardian."

"I'm happy to share a secret with you," Soriya whispered to Shiva. He turned toward her and she slammed her head up into his chin. His grip slackened for only a second, but it gave her enough time to free herself from him. She delivered a punch to the gut. Shiva staggered back, and she followed it up with a kick to his right hand. The demon blade skittered across two lanes before stopping.

"It's over," Soriya said, fists clenched and prepped. "You're done."

"Impressive," Shiva replied. He wiped a line of sweat from his skin. "Ineffective, but impressive nonetheless."

"I'll show you ineffective, you son of a bitch." Soriya slammed her fist into his cheek, followed by another. She drove him back with each hit, but he never fell. He simply laughed.

On the fifth blow, her fist hit his waiting palm. He squeezed and she immediately felt cartilage start to crack from the pressure. Shiva threw her arm down, then delivered an uppercut that sent Soriya soaring. She landed a few feet away with a loud thud against the ground.

"My way will transform the world for the better," Shiva said. He loomed over her. "Accept your fate."

Soriya wasn't looking at him though. She was looking past him and smiled. "Accept yours."

Soriya rolled to her left, pushing off the pavement with everything she had to put distance between her and Shiva. The god, confused at her action, suddenly noticed the light on the ground and where it was coming from.

It was from the truck barreling toward him.

"You—"

The truck hit him straight on. For a second, time stood still and the grill of the pickup caved in from the impact. Then, Shiva flew away into a nearby dump truck. He collapsed beside it.

Soriya rolled to her side and had to blink hard to see through the headlights of the truck. The driver turned them off. She rolled down the window and waved.

"Kali?" Soriya called to the woman behind the wheel.

The goddess smiled as she pointed to the fallen demon blade. "Well, kid? Let's finish this bastard already!"

CHAPTER THIRTY-FIVE

The sword was loose. Everyone who had come to stop Shiva's plans stared at the glinting black of the blade on the pavement. The weapon was the key to everything. Soriya was too far away. She realized it immediately. Working her way to her feet, she ran her hand along her throat. Shiva's grip had left scratches on her skin that felt raw. She shuffled ahead, though her balance was still off from their fight.

Mentor was the closest of them all. He held a hand over his knee, forcing the injured leg ahead with each step. All he had to do was grab the sword and keep it away from Shiva.

Unfortunately, he wasn't fast enough. Shiva shoulder-checked Mentor in the side. The aging teacher put all his weight on his right leg and nearly crashed back to the ground. He fought to maintain his footing, then swung back to knock Shiva aside. The impact caused Shiva to miss the blade completely.

Mentor dove for the weapon. His hand bumped into the hilt accidentally and the sword spun farther from him. He reached for it once more, but Shiva was already there stretching for the demon blade. Excitement danced in his eyes. The light shone brighter in his glassy orbs as Shiva took hold of the sword.

"It's over."

"The hell it is," Mentor said. He kicked off the ground and tackled Shiva. His right fist plowed into the god's gut before Mentor's left hand shot to his kidney—if the deity even had a kidney. None of the blows truly affected Shiva, they were simply delaying tactics. The god laughed as the two wrestled in the dark of the expressway.

Soriya watched it all unfold, paralyzed. The struggle had all happened in a matter of seconds, so fast that her eyes had barely had time to blink and her mind barely had time to process her next move.

Thankfully, Kali was at her side. Her hand nudged Soriya forward. "Get in there, Soriya. He needs you."

Mentor did need her help. All it took was a single backhand from Shiva to send Mentor reeling. Blood flew from his lips. He held his ground, but it didn't matter. Shiva caught his clumsy counterattack and threw him away. Mentor stumbled backward and fell to the ground. Shiva kicked him aside. Mentor rolled along the gravel until he came to a halt. He stayed there, face down in the road, unmoving.

"Mentor…"

"You have to stop Shiva," Kali called, though her voice sounded like a whisper against the beating of Soriya's heart. "He's going for the blade."

"I'm… It's too far. I won't get there in time."

Kali grabbed Soriya's arm and lifted it up. "The ribbon."

"What?"

She didn't understand. Shiva was near the blade. With it in hand he would take out the city, the world. Every sinner, no matter how small the infraction, would be wiped from the face of the earth. Shiva wouldn't transform the future as he believed. He would end it and she was too far away to do anything about it.

"Use the ribbon, Soriya," Kali said.

"I don't—"

"Trust in it," Kali pressed. She held Soriya's arm out, aiming the ribbon toward the target. Her purple irises begged for Soriya to hear her words, to understand. "Trust in me!"

Soriya nodded, then stared down the length of her arm. She focused on the ribbon, on the tendrils snaked along her skin. They loosened with only a thought and snapped ahead like a whip. Two thin lines soared the distance and wrapped tight around Shiva's wrists. His fingertips grazed the hilt of the blade—right before the ribbon pulled the god away from his prize.

"What is this?" he bellowed.

Soriya asked the same thing, but her trust outweighed her curiosity. The ribbon responded to her thoughts, to her need, and dragged Shiva kicking away from the demon blade. He fought against her, and more strands shot out from the line, snagging his ankles while securing their position along his wrists to prevent his escape.

"This… will not… stop me," Shiva said, struggling for freedom.

"It doesn't have to," Mentor replied. He was on his feet and at the blade. He lifted the black steel with both hands.

They had done it. Soriya turned to thank Kali for her help. She stopped short at the sight of the goddess' wide eyes. Kali's hand covered her trembling lips.

"Oh, no," Kali whispered.

"What is it?"

"Wait!" Kali yelled to Mentor.

Mentor didn't hear her cry. He was too focused on the threat before him. "Maybe this will be enough to finish you."

He pulled the blade back, then shot it forward. Obsidian steel sank into Shiva's chest and out his back. White light sparked like flames from his eyes. The god fell to his knees just as Soriya's ribbon retracted, no longer needed to contain the monster.

"Don't," Kali muttered, though the warning was far too late. She raced toward Mentor and Soriya followed. "No, no…"

"Mentor, are you—?"

"I am fine," he answered his student with a look of contentment. "It's over."

Shiva laughed. The sound rang in their ears like a death-knell.

"That doesn't sound good," Soriya said. "Why doesn't that sound good?"

Kali shook her head, hand to her brow. "I didn't know. Didn't realize."

"What, Kali?" Mentor asked.

"We just gave him what he wanted," she said. They stared blankly at her and she pointed to Shiva. The god grabbed the hilt of the sword and buried the blade deeper into his chest.

"Don't you see?"

Shiva smiled. White eyes filled with black ink. His entire body grew dark. "I won."

CHAPTER THIRTY-SIX

The end had finally arrived.

Shiva felt it the moment the demon blade pierced his flesh. The obsidian steel dug deep into his chest, tearing away muscle and sinew as if it had been tissue paper. Every instinct begged for him to scream at the pain coursing through the wound. The agony spread to the very tips of his being.

Instead, Shiva laughed.

They didn't understand. They couldn't fathom his intentions. Shiva had lived with his destiny for millennia. It was a fate he prayed for each and every night. Brahma and the others meditated on the purity of a world that had never existed. Only Shiva had seen the truth in humanity, and he was the only one who knew how to cleanse it.

The black shimmered before him. Slowly, the darkness of the demon blade shifted toward him. His body became the incubator as the sin he'd drained from his victims filled him and spread like a cancer in his dying body. Once purified, the pristine, silver blade fell to the ground and shattered.

It had served its purpose. The seed taken at the docks, nurtured at the temple and the prison, now swelled within him. Sin billowed like heat across his body, which pulsed blue but grew darker with each labored breath. Shiva felt the power inside him. It bubbled along his skin and caused his laughter to die out as his throat was cut off from the last remnants of oxygen in his system.

Shiva closed his eyes and bowed his head in prayer. He gave a silent thanks to the world, for allowing him to complete his sacred task. He prayed for the coming dawn of a changed world, purified of the sin that had infected humanity from the beginning. He would rid the earth of her imperfection and in so doing transform the future. A brighter day awaited all and they would sing Shiva's praises for all time.

The Raktabija was coming.

The blue was no longer present on his body. His skin had turned to black. The infection penetrated even his eyes, and all light from the world faded from view. His body boiled from the demon growing inside him.

Still he smiled. For all the pain, for all the sacrifice required, Shiva would never change a thing. This was his destiny and always had been. The world was changing. His end brought it about. It was a fitting and a noble end, especially if it meant the sanctity of those that survived the great purge.

Through the dim haze of darkness that swallowed the light of the world around him, Shiva caught a glimpse of his killer. The guardian's terror was palpable, his eyes wide at having brought the Raktabija into the world rather than ending the threat. The protector screamed, but her words were lost. She had failed to stop anything. She had failed to see the truth before them.

And Kali?

Her sadness brought joy to Shiva. She had fought her destiny almost as much as he had rushed toward his. She stood as his love and his enemy, his opposite and his better half all in one. They were entwined in destiny, but she could not face it—could not accept that the world did not owe them anything. It would only ever take what it required when the time arose. They played a part in something bigger, and they were only cogs in the wheel of fate.

Sadness turned to recognition in Kali's eyes. It was the last thing Shiva ever saw. His skin bubbled, boiling beneath the surface. The sin was cooking him alive, using his essence like an appetizer. Portents was the meal to come.

His own sin slipped into the growing demon, and his shell was shattered by the transformation. The world was about to change forever and his destiny was fulfilled.

Shiva died happily at that final thought.

CHAPTER THIRTY-SEVEN

Kali should have seen it coming. If she had faced Shiva the moment he had arrived, she might have been able to prevent it. She might have been able to understand the truth behind Shiva's plan and convinced him to stop.

Instead, Kali had run away from everything. She ran from her destiny, and from her fate, but mostly from her own terror, all in the hopes that it would simply disappear. That was the rationale of a child, of a stubborn fool so terrified to face reality until it was far too late. The truth crashed down upon her in the darkness of the RDJ Expressway.

Shiva boiled before them. His body, which once beamed blue like the brightest sky, had turned to char and ash. He was black as night—black like the blade that was stuck through his torso. Only, the blade was no longer obsidian. His body had absorbed the sin collected from the deaths he had caused during his short stay in Portents. His body took in every ounce of darkness, exactly as he had planned.

The demon blade shattered against the pavement. It was no longer of any use to them. It had fulfilled its purpose and played its part in the drama Shiva had started with his arrival.

"What do you mean that was what he wanted?" Mentor asked.

Shiva's smile was the last part of him that melted away. His entire body collapsed in on itself, a mass of black goo on the street. Kali couldn't look away. Her terror locked her in place.

Soriya spun Kali away from the darkness, hand tight to her arm. "Kali. We stopped him, didn't we?"

171

"No," Kali said. "You didn't. He was waiting for you here. He goaded you into this fight."

"What's happening, Kali?" Soriya asked. "What is he doing?"

The black puddle grew. It bubbled and spread out along the ground. The trio backed away, faster and faster, trying to avoid the massive tendrils shooting from the goo. Each strand took shape in the thick black, building up until it towered over them.

"This is exactly what I said would happen, Soriya," Kali explained. "The demon blade was merely a tool. Shiva was the host, a receptacle for the sin infecting the world."

"Now it's unleashed," Mentor said.

Soriya nodded, finally understanding. "The demon you mentioned."

Kali had tried to get Soriya to see the danger to come. Her warning had been meant to scare Soriya off. All it had done was drive Soriya forward, forcing this end for all of them.

"The Raktabija," Kali confirmed. "It's here."

The monster, the demon spawn birthed by sin, loomed over them like a massive wave. The black mass took shape and gained form. It grew enormous hands along the sides. Fingers stretched out and swatted aside the closest street light. The pillar collapsed and the light shattered.

"Soriya," Mentor called, back-pedaling faster.

Kali pointed to the pick-up truck in the distance. "We have to go. Now!"

All agreed and broke into a run for the vehicle. Soriya stuck close to Mentor, helping alleviate some of the burden to his right knee. Kali juggled the keys in her grip.

"How do we stop it?" Soriya asked. Behind them, the Raktabija formed legs. A face took shape in the darkness, eyes blinking to life. "Kali? How do we—?"

"Here," Kali said. She tossed the keys at Soriya. The teen let go of Mentor to catch them. Soriya stopped, staring at the object along her palm.

"What is this?" She held them out. "You drive!"

Mentor circled the truck. He passed the crumpled front bumper and opened the passenger door. "More fleeing for our lives and less arguing, please."

Soriya stared in disbelief. Kali shrugged, then clamored onto the bed of the truck. Soriya huffed and clutched the keys tight before finally hopping inside.

The truck roared to life and Soriya shifted to drive. "Mentor, I—"

Behind them the Raktabija bellowed. It took its first step forward. The demon passed another streetlight which disappeared into its growing mass.

Mentor shook his head. All time for discussion had ended. He pointed ahead. "Floor it, little one."

CHAPTER THIRTY-EIGHT

There were miracles in the world. Circumstances that went above and beyond the possible. True and honest wonders existed for those who were willing to open their eyes and believe. Ruiz had witnessed one that very evening; he had seen it in the scrunched-up face of the little person cradled in his arms.

"Angela," he whispered to the sleeping newborn. He walked carefully through the confines of the hospital room with the name always on his lips. "My little angel."

She was his miracle, his hope for the world rolled up in a swaddling blanket. He swayed through the room. All exhaustion left him. Only joy remained and the serenity of the moment.

From her bed, Michelle beamed at him. She was radiant in spite of the incredible pain she'd gone through only a few hours earlier. She had suffered through labor with a smile on her face thanks to his hand in hers. They had pulled through Angela's birth together, the way it was always meant to be. It was what he had promised when they had gotten married. Those had been simpler times, before he knew about doors to other worlds and stones capable of closing them through sheer force of will. It was a time before monsters in the dark and mayhem in the streets—a time of innocence greatly missed.

Ruiz regained a small piece of that innocence with every gaze at the life in his hands.

"It looks good on you," Michelle said. She shifted uncomfortably on the bed. She snatched another pillow from her side and jammed it behind her. Ruiz moved to assist, but was immediately rebuffed with a wave. Michelle settled against the cushion and sighed. "Even after all these years."

"What?" Ruiz said with a smile. "Five o'clock shadow and a bout of insomnia?"

"Fatherhood."

Angela gurgled and tucked in even closer to his chest. Ruiz reached for his wife and took her hand. "Only because of you."

The peace of the night wouldn't last. Angela would wake in a few minutes and scream bloody murder for a meal. That pattern would carry on for what would seem like years. But right now, Ruiz cherished the silence and the power one tiny infant held over him. Angela Ruiz somehow offered a light at the end of the tunnel.

"I know we were worried," Michelle said, squeezing his hand. She pulled him back to the room and away from the troubled thoughts that crept along the periphery. "But seeing her with you, with us, it's almost like it was meant to be, you know?"

"Yeah," he replied. "Yeah, I do."

He let Michelle's hand go and turned for the window. The Portents skyline stretched across the view and lit up the night outside. Michelle was right. Angela completed their family somehow. She was a missing piece they never realized had been lost in the shuffle of their everyday lives. They had worried for so long. Two daughters had seemed to be enough chaos, so was it really right to bring another life into the mix? That had been Michelle's concern. His ran much deeper thanks to the darkness outside and the terrors that hid around every corner.

There was a killer in the city. He hadn't heard from the precinct all day. He knew that would only last another few hours. He had to find out if his detectives had any news about the temple scene or how it was connected to the slaughter at the docks.

Portents called to him in the quiet. It demanded his help, his service to keep her safe. The city's call started with a flicker in the distance. The expressway, only five blocks away, wrapped through the city like a snake. Lights ran along the road despite the construction that had closed the RDJ off from all traffic.

At least, it should have been closed off from all traffic. A lone truck barreled down the road and headed deeper into the city. Its path appeared erratic, dodging traffic cones and torn-up pavement in the never-ending construction project.

As the truck raced ahead, the lights behind it blinked out. One by one, they were consumed by the night. Ruiz shifted closer, squinting for a better look.

"What is—?" he started, but swallowed the question before Michelle heard him.

Was it an electrical issue? Was it part of the project that had failed to make it in the paper? No, this was something else completely. It was like a mass of darkness was chasing the pick-up truck along the RDJ. The darkness was quickly gaining on the fleeing vehicle.

It was another monster—another threat to the city. Portents begged for him to reply.

"Alejo?" Michelle called. "Is everything okay?"

Ruiz continued to stare at the growing darkness that swept across the expressway. Then he peered down at the life in his hands. He was where he had to be tonight. He had his task in hand, and he had no intention of giving it up.

Reaching for the curtains, Ruiz covered the window. Then he smiled at his wife. "Perfect. Everything is absolutely perfect."

He rocked Angela lightly, careful to keep her safe and secure for as long as possible. The darkness would come later. For now, he was there for her.

Portents was on its own.

CHAPTER THIRTY-NINE

The tires squealed as the truck veered to the left to avoid another torn-up lane. Soriya floored the pedal, forcing the struggling pick-up to zoom even faster along the expressway. It happened each time she checked her mirrors. The Raktabija was gaining on them.

The demon trudged ahead, each step bringing it that much closer to them. No matter where the truck turned, no matter the speed, the monster continued to gain ground. They were quickly running out of options. Roadblocks lined the left side of the street. Cones barred the exits on the right. Soriya's choices were growing more and more limited.

Her company wasn't much in the way of help.

"Hands at ten and two," Mentor said. He held tight to the dash with his leg braced as if a collision was imminent.

"Are you kidding me right now?" Soriya asked, astonished. She hadn't wanted the keys *or* the responsibility of driving them to safety. Why any sixteen-year-old would was a question that deserved further study at a later date. She was too busy hoping she wouldn't blow a tire by hopping steep curbs left in the road. "You're going to question my driving? Now?"

"Eyes on the road," he said, pointing ahead. "Eyes on the road!"

Soriya spun the wheel to the right. The truck narrowly avoided a row of cones she had failed to notice on her left side. Her chest heaved, and she was afraid to even blink for fear of missing something else.

Kali chuckled under her breath from her seat against the

back of the cab. The window separating them was open and she peered inside. Her smile caused Soriya's jaw to clench.

"And you thought my lesson was stressful?"

"It was," Soriya snapped, wrapping her fingers around the wheel even tighter. "And so is this."

"How bad is it?" Mentor asked. Soriya turned to answer, then stopped when she realized he was looking behind them. Soriya had her own answer, though the question had been passed to Kali. The black mass barreled after them, and the streetlights continued to blink out from the sides of the road. Yet even with complete blackness, Soriya could see the eyes of the Raktabija.

The demon was hungry.

Kali grimaced. "Very bad, Stony." She patted Soriya's shoulder. "Speed it up, kid."

She couldn't. Speed was no longer an option. The truck shook from their current pace—the speedometer had maxed out at 70. If the borrowed conveyance had been a modern vehicle, or even one without recent impact damage, more speed might have been viable. The junker Kali had managed to procure to save their asses, however, was failing them.

Mentor glanced up at the dash and then at Soriya's feet. He read her look of concern. "What can this thing do exactly? This Raktabija?"

"Everything the demon blade could," Kali said, shouting over the whipping wind and the angry cries of the monster behind them. "With one touch the Raktabija will swallow up the sins of the world and any who committed them."

"Mentor, that's—"

"Millions," Mentor finished. "You're talking about millions of people."

"Just in Portents," Kali said. "If this thing gets out into the world?"

Mentor ran his fingers through his beard. "He's wiping the slate clean. Shiva's transforming the planet as he always intended."

Kali nodded. No words were necessary. Shiva's destiny was being played out in real time. He had achieved the fate he had sought his entire life.

The truck hit a bump in the road and bounced up. Road-blocks boxed her in, forcing the truck through a thin gap.

"How do we stop it?" She had to ask, though the initial reaction from Kali was enough to make her regret it. She'd heard the excuses throughout the last day, ever since Kali had brought Shiva to their attention. Kali had believed him to be too powerful and that there was nothing they could do against him. Shiva, however, was no longer part of the equation and something had to be done to stop the Raktabija. *She* had to do something. The demon was in her city, and now it was her responsibility. Soriya meant to stand and fight with everything she had left.

Still, Kali remained silent. Stray glances flashed back to the creature, then to her companion. Soriya slammed on the horn to draw her attention.

"Kali!" she shouted. "I need an idea or some kind of solution. I'm running out of road. The construction…"

The roadblocks opened up to four lanes again as the RDJ curved away from downtown for the Riverside district. It should have continued for another three miles before dropping them at the eastern border of the city. Unfortunately, the next bridge was out. Since the area was cordoned off, with gates on the exits and vehicles that barricaded anyone from advancing, they had run out of road.

"What can we do, Kali?"

Kali closed her eyes and took a deep breath as Soriya continued to surge ahead. They could travel for only another minute before crashing. Soriya looked around for an exit, but all ways were obstructed. She couldn't see any options.

Kali's hand fell on Soriya's shoulder once more. She squeezed lightly. Soriya used the rearview mirror to catch a glimpse of the woman.

Kali was smiling. "Only one thing we can do."

It was in her eyes. Even with the smile, and the cocksure attitude in the goddess' words, Soriya saw the sadness in Kali's purple irises.

Mentor was the first to speak though. "Kali…"

"It's all right, Stony."

"What is?" Soriya asked, unwilling to let the thought take root. "What's all right?"

"Turn us around, Soriya."

"No," the teen said. She looked ahead, demanding an option to open up. Her thoughts begged—screamed—for something to come to light and save them. "I—"

"Soriya," Kali said. "It's time for me to face my fate."

CHAPTER FORTY

"No."

None of them wanted to admit it. Kali led the pack in that regard, though it had been her suggestion. The time had come to stop running and face the menace behind them. Soriya had asked her to do that ever since their first meeting. Now Soriya was the defiant one.

"I won't do it," she said.

"Soriya, there's no time," Mentor chimed in, though worry was rampant on his face. He didn't care for the plan either. Hell, there wasn't much of a plan at all, more like the Hail Mary to end all Hail Mary's—to which Kali couldn't help but chuckle at the reference. If they failed to stop the Raktabija now, Portents would be lost. More accurately, the people of Portents would be lost. The city would become a ghost town, leaving only the innocent to fend for themselves when the infrastructure collapsed around them.

Portents was only the first stop in a worldwide all-you-can-eat buffet for the demon. Billions were at risk. They had run out of options.

"I'm not going to let her throw her life away!" Soriya shouted. She was ever the protector—always carrying so much strength for all those around her. Kali had made her question her role as the Greystone, and for that she should have apologized. If nothing else, she had come to recognize the weight of the job as the ultimate motivation for the teen. Soriya thrived in the role and had made it her own. How could Kali have ever thought her weak for caring about those around her? How could she have ever put Soriya in danger like she had?

"It's my life, Soriya," Kali said. "It's my decision to make."

"Stop," Soriya said. She shook her head, squeezing the steering wheel with all her strength. They closed on the bridge quickly. They didn't have anywhere else to go except head on into the pylons and barricades dividing the zones. Still, Soriya sped ahead. "We can think of something. I *have* to think of something."

Kali's head bowed. She understood the teen's reluctance. This wasn't an easy decision to make. Ever since she'd caught sight of Shiva at the docks, Kali had done everything to avoid playing his game. It had always been about fate. She swore never to fall into that trap, never to believe in something so wholeheartedly that it was all-consuming. She had wanted to live and be someone. She had wanted to exist.

The cost had become too high to allow that to continue. Even Mentor realized it. He turned toward the window, lost to the darkness racing after them.

"Mentor," Soriya said, her voice almost pleading with her teacher for an answer. "We can find a way. You have to see that, right? We can find some way out of this, some way to stop that thing. Right?"

He said nothing.

"*This* is the way, Soriya," Kali answered for him.

"It's not, Kali. I won't—"

"She isn't throwing her life away," Mentor explained. Sullen eyes met Kali's and he nodded to her with silent thanks. "She's saving us all."

"Same as you would," Kali said.

The barricade closed in on them. Soriya screamed as she let her foot off the accelerator and slammed on the brake. The truck slowed. Soriya spun the wheel, tires squealing as the pickup turned to avoid the barricade at the edge of the bridge.

Everyone took a breath. Quietly, Soriya shifted into reverse and brought the truck around. The Raktabija stole the light from the RDJ, yet the outline of the creature was clear. He towered over them, a black mass of hate and sin that stood more than eighty feet tall. Darkness swirled in shapes: a mouth and two eyes—screaming at them.

"My God," Mentor muttered.

"Ugly son of a bitch, ain't he?" Kali commented.

"What are you going to do?" Soriya asked.

"What I should have done from the start," Kali replied. "What I've always had to do."

"Kali—"

Kali shook her head, silencing Soriya. "When I tell you, turn the wheel and get the hell out of here. You got me?"

Soriya didn't answer. She looked toward her teacher, who nodded. He didn't have to tell her the truth. There were no options. There was no last-minute rescue, no hope that good would triumph. There was only the choice Kali had given them.

"You've got a job to do, Soriya," Kali said. "And you're going to be great at it. I know you are. This one, though? This one is mine."

Soriya swiped at watery eyes. She shifted to drive and hit the gas. The truck jerked forward and sped toward the monster. The Raktabija raged, rushing directly for them. Lights blinked out and tendrils shot from its black mass in an attempt to reach them. Soriya didn't slow.

"Ready?" Soriya asked. Mentor held tighter to the dash. The Raktabija loomed closer and closer.

"Not yet!" Kali yelled. She stood in the back of the truck, steady breaths calming her. "Keep going!"

Darkness consumed the expressway. Shadow swallowed the light ahead of them. Soriya sped up. When there was nothing left but the black mass of the beast before them, Kali yelled to them.

"Now!"

Soriya slammed on the brake and spun the wheel. Kali took a running start across the bed of the truck. The vehicle turned away from the creature and started back toward the bridge. Before it could, Kali leapt at the Raktabija.

The demon devoured her whole.

Darkness swept over her. Tendrils ensnared her arms and locked her in place. Kali felt her body disappear into its thick mass. The Raktabija consumed her. The sins of the world, the shadows of the universe, filled her and made her one with them.

It had been everything she had run from in her life. Her fate, her destiny. She had fled from the end of her story, drowning herself in the emptiness of revelry without purpose—without a path ahead. There was only joy and it had held no meaning whatsoever. Not to her and not to anyone around her. She had never aspired for anything, and had never achieved anything. She had merely existed.

The Raktabija bellowed its victory.

All Kali could do was smile. She opened her mouth and took a deep breath. She drew the sin surrounding her inside. She swallowed the black tendrils and everything that came with it. The demon believed her to be the meal. He had it backwards.

Kali sucked in every last drop of the monster, at last fulfilling her destiny as the true destroyer. She continued, fighting through the pain and the eventual death that would take her. All to heal the world, to save the day.

The way a teenager named Soriya Greystone had taught her.

CHAPTER FORTY-ONE

It felt like a lifetime had passed. Every lurch, every shift of the creature seemed to carry over for an eternity, yet only seconds passed in the interim. The truck coasted along the expressway, and Soriya kept her eyes locked on the rearview mirror instead of the road ahead. Eventually she hit the brake and put the vehicle in park. It was a mindless task. Soriya was unconscious to all but the darkness behind them.

The demon stretched across all eight lanes of the RDJ. A shimmering black mouth widened with elation. The Raktabija had won. It had killed Kali.

It took a step forward, black-tendril hands raised in triumph. Soriya didn't budge, didn't move for the shifter. Her hands remained on the wheel, but she couldn't continue to run. She couldn't, not with her friend lost inside the beast.

"Soriya," Mentor called. His voice was little more than a whisper. He sounded miles away compared to the inches he truly was. "We should keep driving. We don't know if Kali was able to stop the Raktabija. We don't know if she even had the a chance before…"

He trailed off. The outcome didn't have to be mentioned. Neither of them had to say the word to feel it in their hearts. Kali had leapt into the beast. She had sacrificed herself to save them—to give them the chance to escape. More than that, it was to face her fate.

Soriya had fought against the decision. Death was never the outcome one desired, not when it came to those she cared for: friends and connections she had made during her life. Death was, however, the reality. No matter how much it pained her.

Kali was gone and the beast remained. It continued to devour the light from the lamps adorning the side of the road. The demon pressed forward, pushing toward the spires of downtown. If the Raktabija reached the city, millions would die.

As it shifted closer and closer to the car, Soriya tensed in her seat. They needed to run. They needed to get off the highway and warn as many people as they could. Their words would have no effect, they would sound like the rantings of lunatics, but it was the only play left to them.

Then the Raktabija paused.

Slowly, Soriya's hands left the wheel and she reached for her door. "Wait."

"Soriya…"

The door opened, and the rush of wind pushed her hair from her face. She stood in the cold and stared into the shadows that made up the demon. The monster's hands fell from above. Fists that had been clenched in victory opened and the Raktabija's fingers spread like claws around his midsection. The screams of triumph changed to those of pain.

"It's… I think it's working," Soriya said.

Mentor opened his door to join her. The creature was so close they could feel the darkness reaching out to them, almost pulling them in. Mentor's hand fell on her shoulder.

"Come on, Soriya, we have to—"

"Look!"

The black mass started to shrink before their eyes. Tendrils that once expanded to all sides, as well as the darkness that towered before them, receded. The demon's scream filled the night as the shadows were sucked into the center of the mass.

Those screams echoed when the Raktabija fell. Arms collapsed and shattered on each side. The demon's legs dwindled to sticks before snapping. The mass at the center, however, was the important part. It was where Soriya focused. The Raktabija imploded and caved in on itself as its mass was pulled in—drawn in—by the woman lost in the heart of the monster.

Kali fell to the pavement. The demon was gone. Her body lay in a heap, her back to them. She didn't move. She didn't breathe.

Soriya broke into a run. Mentor, desperate to hold her back, lost his grip. "Wait! Soriya, don't! You don't know what—"

She didn't. She didn't know anything beyond that her friend was hurt, but more importantly that there was a chance to save her.

She slid behind Kali, knees scraping on the pavement. Her hand hovered over the woman's bare arm. Beneath the skin, the tendrils of the Raktabija spread out like a cancer. "No. Kali…"

The darkness flowed through her body, then faded from view. As the last remnants dissipated beneath the surface, Kali gasped for breath. Soriya stumbled back, then shot forward once more. She pulled her friend close and patted her back to clear her airway.

"Hey," she said. "You're okay. You're going to be okay."

Kali's eyes fluttered. They struggled to remain open. Her pupils were dilated and black filled the white space. With each blink, as each breath left her, the purple returned to her irises.

Her eyes widened in terror and Kali pulled away from Soriya. She pounded at her chest. In one large burst, Kali let out a burp that echoed in the silence of the road.

Kali shook her head and stuck out her tongue in disgust. "Excuse me," she said, continuing to pat her chest. "That was gross."

Mentor joined them. "Is she okay? What was that?"

Soriya laughed. "Demon burp."

"So nasty," Kali remarked. Soriya stood and helped Kali to her feet. "Thanks."

"The Raktabija," Mentor said. "Is it—?"

Kali nodded. "It's gone. Yeah." She rubbed at her chest. "Unless you count the *major* heartburn going on right now."

Mentor rolled his eyes. His irritation helped to hide his relief, but Soriya knew him too well. Her smile was locked in place and she nudged close to Kali.

"How about a drink to put out that fire?" Soriya asked her friend. She was proud of Kali's sacrifice, proud Kali had taken a stand after running for so long.

Kali didn't care about any of that, though. The second she

heard the word drink, her ears perked up, and her hand clasped tight to Soriya's. "I knew there was a reason I liked you."

Their laughter carried them back to the truck.

CHAPTER FORTY-TWO

The dull hum of the Bypass filled Soriya's ears. The green glow soothed her tired body. She wanted to collapse, wanted to put everything behind her, and pray she had the strength to do it all again tomorrow.

That had been the worry, the concern at the heart of things. The burden of the job weighed on her like never before. But she stuck with it, and she pushed herself to act. It was the way Mentor had taught her for so long. It was the only way she knew. The choice had been hers and no one else's. No fate, no destiny, merely the perseverance of a child who now stood on the cusp of adulthood with a mission.

It was a mission she would never surrender, never cast aside. The work was too important. For the sake of Portents and everyone within her borders. Hell, after tonight, she could believe the *world* benefited from her role to some degree.

Kali joined her in the light of the Bypass. She was the first guest ever welcomed into the chamber as far as Soriya recalled. To Mentor, their home was sacred; their task to keep the Bypass safe was too important to allow outsiders to view it, let alone be aware of its presence in the first place.

The invitation was made so she could keep watch over Kali. The moment they arrived, however, all attention turned to Soriya's shoulder wound. She had fought against the poking and prodding from her new friend, but eventually relented. She pulled her shirt away from her right shoulder and allowed the goddess a closer look.

Kali grazed the wound with her fingers, then dug a little with her thumb inside. Curses slipped from Soriya, but she didn't pull away. Kali removed her thumb and stuck the tip between her lips.

A smirk escaped her. "The infection is gone."

"I could have told you that," Soriya replied. She fixed her shirt, then stretched out her arm to spread out the pain.

"I had to be sure."

Soriya nodded. "So no demons hiding in there?"

"Just the usual ones," Kali answered. They shared a laugh, then fell silent. They had both seen their share of darkness over the last day, thanks to the Raktabija. To know a small piece of that monster had been in Soriya, that sin had the power to overwhelm even the purest of souls, frightened her.

Now Kali was drowning in it all. She said nothing, and never gave away an inkling of her suffering, but Soriya recognized it plain as day. It was in the distant stares from her as she stood before the Bypass. It was in the quiet held between them, something Kali had never seemed comfortable with. She had always pushed for frivolity in Portents; she always needed the contentment that came from losing herself in a crowd.

Kali shifted beyond the pillars holding the Bypass in place, then held out her hand before the spinning green of the floating orb.

"What about you, Kali?" Soriya finally asked, though the question made the moment all too real for her. She had tried to ignore it for so long, ever since she had run to Kali's side in the aftermath of their struggle against the Raktabija. She wanted to hold onto the fun of their adventure, the light, the jokes, and even the danger that came from being around Kali. But reality crept in, and it fought to remind Soriya of what came next, what would always come next—be it a day, a decade, or more, for all of them.

"You told me if you stopped the demon, if you fulfilled your destiny, it would be the end of you."

"Soriya…"

"You look okay," Soriya continued. Her words strained in her throat, her tone timid against the truth. "You look fine to me, like—"

"I can feel it, Soriya," Kali said without looking. She crept closer to the veil, but never pierced the Bypass. Her hand ran along its surface, dancing along the light of the infinite void trapped within. "It's this churning inside my guts, building with each breath. The change is coming and I can't stop it. I never could."

"Why then?" Soriya asked, anger in the question. Anger at herself for not stopping Kali from acting. Anger at not being strong enough to handle things on her own. "Why did you do it?"

"I had to," Kali said. She turned to face Soriya, a sad smile on her face. "You showed me that, Soriya. This is what I was meant for, my role, and I wouldn't have it any other way. You were right. I was afraid to face my fate. Now... Now I don't have to be."

Soriya tried to smile. She tried to see the light in what Kali said. She had hoped to find someone to share her burden with, to work with to keep the city safe. She had inspired Kali to do just that. It should have filled her with pride, but her friend was dying before her eyes—changing into someone else—and would soon be lost forever. Soriya swiped at her eyes.

"Hey now," Kali said. She stepped away from the Bypass and pulled Soriya close for a hug. "None of that."

"I know. It's just—"

Kali shook her head. "Not today. After all, it's still your birthday."

The ribbon, Kali's gift to her, snaked tighter to Soriya's arm. Soriya pulled at the ends, feeling the softness of the fabric around her skin. The ribbon was a part of Kali she would never lose, a piece of her spirit and her grace that would stay by her side long after the end.

"It doesn't feel like much of a birthday," Soriya said. She started for her room, which was tucked in the corner of the chamber. She didn't get far before she noticed a shadow at the bottom of the stairs.

"Let's see what we can do to change that," Mentor called. He carried a pizza in his hands. On top was a six-pack for their guest. "Happy birthday, Soriya."

Kali snatched up both the food and booze. She slipped inside the small domicile. When she returned she had a beer opened already. She held it before them.

"To many more, Soriya."

Mentor ushered her inside. The fireplace roared and so did their laughter. Stories were shared as they ate. The danger was in the past and they bonded over their shared struggles, both those overcome and those yet to be.

Soriya fell silent and devoured her promised birthday dinner with zeal. She watched the two imposing figures before her. Their stories bordered on arguments on more than one occasion. They brought a smile to her face.

For all the burden, for all the trials, Soriya was grateful to have them at her side. Not only them, but the others she had managed to connect with in her short existence. Beth, Urg, Kok'-Kol—so many strange and unique creatures and people she prided herself in knowing. They stood at her side, fought with her and for her. They were the inspiring ones, the ones she couldn't be prouder to be around.

Soriya realized how blessed she truly had been in her life. She would never forget that, not for as long as she lived.

CHAPTER FORTY-THREE

The celebration had ended an hour earlier. Soriya, exhausted from the day, had passed out with a smile on her face. *Sixteen years old.* Mentor treasured every day with her.

When he had arrived, when the laughing and eating started, he'd noticed his gift sitting on the mantel. The small piece of jewelry had haunted him for so long, and it was a truth he had sought to hide from Soriya since their first meeting. No, even before then. He had planned to give the gift to her, to explain the truth and the story told to her to cover it up this whole time. Instead, he held onto the locket. He set the necklace in the wooden chest tucked in the corner of the domicile and locked it inside—along with the truth.

He couldn't do it to her. Not now, not on her birthday. It had been meant to solidify their bond. All the locket would have done, however, was create a rift. All answers from the past would. It had been his fault. He should have been honest from the beginning, wiped the questions from her mind, and told her everything: from his real name to those of her parents. He knew it all and he kept the secrets to himself. He kept *her* for himself.

It was her birthday, though, and she deserved the joy that came with the special occasion. The truth could wait a little longer. Today was about Soriya.

"She's a good kid," Kali said. She looked back at the sleeping teen, then joined Mentor near the pillars of the chamber. "Tough, considering what she's been through."

"Tough on herself most of all," Mentor remarked. He had never realized the burden placed on her. His burden. Especially with his injury at the hands of the Minotaur. Soriya had been young to begin with, and no teenager should have had to shoulder the responsibilities that came with the mantle of the Greystone. His knee had caused him to rely on her more and the stress his new limitation had created weighed her down. But she had been strong. She fought through her doubts and faced the danger. He was proud of her for that, for always being there, not only for the city but for him as well.

"Well, look who she's trying to impress." Kali grinned. It faded quickly as she buckled over slightly, hand gripping tight to her stomach. Her other hand shot out for support from the closest pillar. She had hidden the pain well during their meal, letting laughter serve as the best medicine. Kali's sacrifice in handling the Raktabija, unfortunately, appeared to be catching up to her.

"How much longer?" he asked, though he was afraid of the answer. The black tendrils shifted under her skin. Her youth, maintained for centuries, suffered as wrinkles ran from her eyes and over her hands.

Kali let go of the pillar and straightened her back. She took a deep breath and closed her eyes. When she opened them, they appeared muted—no longer sharp and ferocious.

"Soon," she muttered. She gazed back at the sleeping teen. "Too soon."

"You should rest." Mentor reached for her. He wanted to research the situation more. There were plenty of texts in his room, as well as plenty of options yet to be explored. To give up and throw in the towel was not something he could do. Not after her sacrifice, not with everything Soriya had shown him over the past day.

"I can't," Kali replied. "Not here."

She moved closer to the Bypass. Her steps were so quick, Mentor nearly jumped to try and stop her; he was afraid she might very well slip right into the glowing green of the infinite. Instead, she held to the veil and her hand ran along the surface. She soaked in the past and the future, a myriad of possibilities.

"When it comes, when I change to this next iteration of Kali, I can't be here. I can't be in this world. I won't risk it." Her head bowed in sadness. "Nothing good comes from me after this."

He wanted to argue. He wanted to pull her back and shake away the melancholy that had consumed the Kali he'd come to know over the years. Her pain-in-the-ass mentality had driven him insane as they'd hunted monsters. Yet, she had always grounded him in a way, despite her origins as a goddess. She was always the more human of the two, living *in* the world instead of separate from it. He wanted to save that, to hold onto her for a moment more, but he couldn't.

"I understand."

"I'm glad I met Soriya though. That I had the chance to spend some time with her."

Mentor grimaced. "The less said about that the better."

"Okay," Kali replied with a laugh. "Maybe not the best lessons to teach her, but some necessary ones for sure."

"She will miss you," Mentor said. "We both will."

Her hand returned to the Bypass, letting the floating orb spin along her skin. They had always had opposing viewpoints, always struggling when forced to work together. After everything, though, he viewed her as a friend. He didn't have many he regarded in such a fashion. He hated the thought of losing one, of seeing one die.

"Don't give me the sourpuss, Stony," Kali chided, catching his ruminations. "There's no reason—"

She stopped. Her eyes widened with awareness and her hand fell back to her side, leaving behind the Bypass and the knowledge stored within.

"Oh," was all she could say.

"Kali?" Mentor asked with concern. "What's wrong?"

"You saw it," she said. She peered at the swirling orb, the question answered in an instant. Not by him, but by the void. The question he never should have asked in the first place, and the one that would haunt him until the end. "You saw your death."

It was the other secret he had planned to share with Soriya. It was the reason behind the locket, and the reason behind his need to divulge the truth to her after obscuring it for so long. He didn't know how much time he had left to make things right.

He had lied about so much, hidden her past from her in the hopes of securing her future. He feared losing Soriya even now, knowing his death was coming.

Mentor nodded, accepting what he had seen.

"Then you know how this ends," Kali said.

They haunted him with every glimpse into the Bypass: those mismatched eyes. They would be the end of him, the last things he would ever see in this world.

"I do."

"No," Kali replied. She stepped over to the aging teacher. A hand grazed his cheek. She turned his attention back to the domicile and the sleeping teen. "I mean for Soriya."

"I…" Gray eyes snapped back to the Bypass. He had never asked, never pushed to know more than what he had seen. His own demise had become a chain tied around his ankles. It was a weight he was now forced to carry on his own. He couldn't imagine anything more painful until Kali mentioned Soriya's fate. "I never thought to—"

"I'm sorry," Kali said, shaking her head. "I shouldn't have said anything."

"Kali…"

Returning to the edge of the Bypass, she faced him one last time. "Thank you for everything. I have to—"

"Wait," Mentor said. "Kali, wait."

"I can't, Stony. It's coming and I—"

"I know. I know it is and I understand, but…" Mentor looked to Soriya, innocent and asleep. She had become his treasured daughter over the last decade. She stood at his side, listened to every word spoken, and fought with every ounce of her being. She had believed in him and trusted in him. He had believed that with the time remaining he could make her ready to face the burden alone, to protect Portents after his death.

But if she fell as well? If there was no one else in line? What happened then?

He couldn't accept *her* end. His own was one thing, but to acknowledge Soriya's death as well? He could never face that.

"What is it, Stony?"

"Before you go I need a favor," he said. Kali read his look and the troubled gaze that followed back to Soriya. "I need one last gift from you."

ABOUT THE AUTHOR

Lou Paduano is the author of the Greystone series of urban fantasy adventures, which follow Detective Greg Loren and Soriya Greystone as they hunt myths, monsters, and legends in the city of Portents.

He is also the author of the conspiracy thriller series, The DSA, a serialized tale about a clandestine government agency trying to discover the true power behind humanity's future.

He lives in Grand Island, New York with his wife and three daughters. Sign up for his e-mail list for free content as well as updates on future releases at loupaduano.com.

THE GREYSTONE SAGA

AVAILABLE NOW

Follow the adventures of Soriya Greystone and
Detective Greg Loren as they hunt dangerous
myths and legends in the city of Portents.

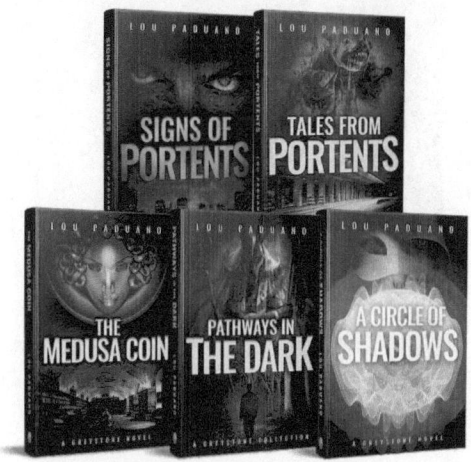

THE DSA SEASON ONE
AVAILABLE NOW

Ben Riley is recruited into a secret government organization and finds himself knee-deep in a mystery that will change the world...

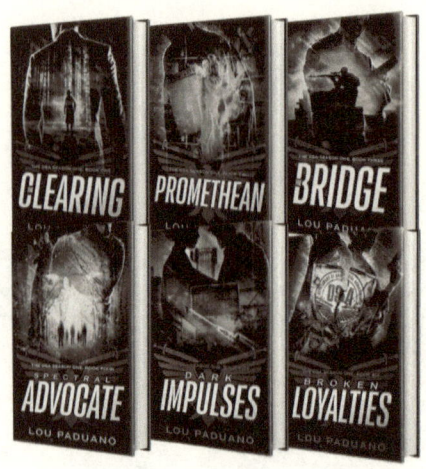

BOOK ONE - THE CLEARING
BOOK TWO - PROMETHEAN
BOOK THREE - THE BRIDGE
BOOK FOUR - SPECTRAL ADVOCATE
BOOK FIVE - DARK IMPULSES
BOOK SIX - BROKEN LOYALTIES

GREYSTONE-IN-TRAINING CONCLUDES IN…

The Daughters of Salem have returned.

A doorway was opened and a threat from the earliest days of Portents has found its way home. The Daughters have a clear mission: to use the power of the doorkeeper and awaken a terrible darkness on the world.

Soriya stands alone to face the threat. To do so, she must protect the magic-wielding doorkeeper—a woman in a desperate search to find her past.

There is more at stake for Soriya, though, as Mentor levels one final test upon her. Should she pass, Soriya will at last earn the mantle of the Greystone.

If she fails, however, all of Portents may succumb to the darkness within their souls.